"You are a bra⸺ Prentiss."

She caught his gaze

"Excuse me?"

"I like it when you call me Olivia."

He took a step closer. "Really?"

She shrugged, trying to make light of her request. "Everybody calls me Vivi. Sometimes it makes me feel six again. Being called Olivia makes me feel like an adult."

"Or a woman."

The way he said *woman* sent heat rushing through her. Once again, he'd seen right through her ploy and might even realize she was attracted to him—

Oh, who was she kidding? He *knew* she was attracted to him.

She stepped back. "I wouldn't go that far."

He caught her hand and tugged her to him. "I would."

He kissed her so quickly that her knees nearly buckled and her brain reeled. She could have panicked. Could have told him to go slow because she hadn't done this in a while, or even stop because this was wrong. But nobody, no kiss, had ever made her feel the warm, wonderful, scary sensations saturating her entire being right now. Not just her body, but her soul.

Dear Reader,

The best thing about writing for the Harlequin Romance line is that the editors aren't afraid to let us tackle some interesting, sometimes difficult topics. In *Daring to Trust the Boss,* I pair Olivia Prentiss, a woman who was bullied at university after trying to prosecute a football hero who attacked her, with billionaire Tucker Engle, a former foster child.

Tucker has done everything Olivia wants to do. He's escaped his past and made something of himself. But what she doesn't realize is he's missing the human connection that Olivia takes for granted in her big, noisy family.

Having come from a large family myself, I found it fascinating to explore the other side of the coin. What would it be like to be alone? Totally alone. And wonder if you would ever fit anywhere?

But flying with Tucker to Italy to help Constanzo Bartulocci find his illegitimate son throws Olivia into a world of glitz and glamour where she's the odd girl out. It seems neither fits in the other's life.

They don't want to fall in love. At times, they don't even want to like each other. But Cupid's got his eye on them and sometimes there's no escaping destiny!

I hope you enjoy Tucker and Olivia's story and our trip to Italy!

Susan

Daring to
Trust the Boss

—

Susan Meier

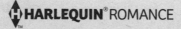
HARLEQUIN® ROMANCE

Recycling programs
for this product may
not exist in your area.

ISBN-13: 978-0-373-74276-9

DARING TO TRUST THE BOSS

First North American Publication 2014

Copyright © 2014 by Linda Susan Meier

Printed in U.S.A.

www.Harlequin.com

Susan Meier spent most of her twenties thinking she was a job-hopper—until she began to write and realized everything that had come before was only research! One of eleven children, with twenty-four nieces and nephews and three kids of her own, Susan has had plenty of real-life experience watching romance blossom in unexpected ways. She lives in western Pennsylvania with her wonderful husband, Mike, three children and two overfed, well-cuddled cats, Sophie and Fluffy. You can visit Susan's website, at www.susanmeier.com.

Also by Susan Meier

SINGLE DAD'S CHRISTMAS MIRACLE
A FATHER FOR HER TRIPLETS+
HER PREGNANCY SURPRISE
THE BILLIONAIRE'S BABY SOS*
NANNY FOR THE MILLIONAIRE'S TWINS**
THE TYCOON'S SECRET DAUGHTER**
KISSES ON HER CHRISTMAS LIST
BABY ON THE RANCH***
SECOND CHANCE BABY***
THE BABY PROJECT***
BABY BENEATH THE CHRISTMAS TREE

+Mothers in a Million series
*Part of The Larkville Legacy
**First Time Dads! duet
***Babies in the Boardroom trilogy

This and other titles by Susan Meier available in ebook format at www.Harlequin.com.

CHAPTER ONE

"I'M OLIVIA PRENTISS, here for my first day in Accounting."

The gray-haired Human Resources director glanced up with a smile. "Good morning, Olivia. Welcome to Inferno." She happily flipped through the files in a box on her desk, but when she found the one with "Olivia Prentiss" written on the tab, she winced. "I'm afraid there's been a change of plans."

Vivi's stomach dropped to the floor. "I'm not hired?"

"No. No. Nothing like that. You've been reassigned temporarily."

"I don't understand."

"Tucker Engle's assistant was in an accident last week."

"Oh. I'm sorry." She knew Tucker Engle was the CEO and chairman of the board of Inferno. Before she'd interviewed for this job, she'd researched the company and his name had popped up. But the company's annual statements had said little about the reclusive billionaire. When she'd searched the internet, she'd only found an interview with the *Wall Street Journal* and a Facebook rant by a former employee who had called him the Grim Reaper because the only time he came out of his ivory tower was to fire someone. Still, none of that information gave her any clue what his assistant's accident had to do with her.

"As the newest employee in the company, it falls to you to stand in for Betsy."

Her already-fallen stomach soured. *She* had to work directly with a guy called the Grim Reaper by his staff?

She gulped. "An accountant stands in for a personal assistant?"

"You won't be a *personal* assistant."

Following the sound of the deep male voice, Vivi swung around. A tall, dark-haired man leaned against the door frame. Her gaze crawled from his shiny black loafers up his black trousers and suit jacket, past his white shirt and sky-blue tie to a pair of emerald-green eyes.

Wow.

"Or even an administrative assistant. You'll be an assistant." He pushed away from the door frame and walked over to her. "The assistant to the chairman of the board. The assistant who must be able to read financial reports and change things I need to have changed. An assistant who has to be able to keep up." His lush mouth thinned. "Do you have a problem with that?"

Intimidation froze her limbs, her tongue, and she could only stare.

"Good." Obviously taking her silence for acceptance, he headed for the door. "Spend the twenty minutes you need with Mrs. Martin to get your ID badge and fill out your paperwork then report to my office."

He strode out and she stared at the empty space he left in his wake.

"He's a whirlwind."

Obviously, Mrs. Martin was paid to say nice things because Vivi wouldn't call him a whirlwind. He was more like a bully. A really good-looking bully, but still a bully.

Bile rose to her throat, but she shoved it down again. She'd dealt with bullies before. "I take it that's Tucker Engle."

"In the gorgeous flesh."

"He demoted me even before I started."

Mrs. Martin shook her head. "It's not a demotion. That's what he was telling you. The assistant job is a lot more than you think it is."

"But I need to start my real job now. I have to keep my skills sharp to take the CPA exam. I don't want to fall behind."

"You'll be working with *the* Tucker Engle. The man who leads Inferno. You'll see everything he does—learn everything he knows."

That didn't mesh with the picture painted in the Facebook rant, but it sounded promising. Like something she could cling to to force herself to be able to work with him. "So he'll teach me things?"

"I don't know about *teaching,* per se." Mrs. Martin motioned for her to sit in the chair in front of her desk. She pointed to a little camera attached to her computer monitor. "Take a seat so I can get your employee picture."

Vivi sat.

"Anyway, I don't know about him teaching you, but you'll learn a lot working with him. He built this company—"

"With help."

"Help?" Mrs. Martin laughed. "You think he had help? Everybody who works here supports *him.* He's the idea man. No one else."

That *did* mesh with what she'd read. In the interview he'd given the *Wall Street Journal*, he'd bragged that he used only accountants, lawyers, PR people—support staff. He didn't want, or need, an equal.

"Fantastic."

Mrs. Martin smiled sympathetically. "I understand you're disappointed. You see this as a setback. And I probably can't talk you out of that." She paused and sucked in a resigned breath. "So, I'm going to stop the sugarcoating and be totally honest with you. Tucker Engle is a suspicious prima donna. He gives assignments piecemeal so that no one can figure out what he's working on. He's so demanding that none of our employees would volunteer to replace Betsy—even for a few weeks."

Her heart stuttered. "And you think *I* can?"

"I didn't pick you. We gave Mr. Engle the files of the accountants starting today and he chose you. Like it or not, you're stuck. But Betsy won't be out forever. Eight weeks—"

Her eyes bulged. "Eight weeks?"

Mrs. Martin grimaced. "Twelve tops."

"Oh, my God!"

"But you still get your accountant's salary. And your time with Mr. Engle counts in your seniority with the company. It's not as if you'll be starting over when Betsy returns."

"No, thanks. I'll just keep my job in Accounting."

Mrs. Martin sighed. "How good do you think it's going to look on your employee records if you refuse your first assignment?"

"It's not the position I was hired for."

"Nonetheless, it's your first assignment and if you don't take it, he may tell us to fire you."

She was really, really sorry she'd found that Facebook rant because she couldn't even argue that. "Of course he will."

Mrs. Martin's face fell into sympathetic lines. "The other option is to quit."

* * *

"The other option is to quit."

Vivi muttered those words under her breath as she made her way through the maze of red-, orange- and yellow-walled corridors, looking for the private elevator to the executive office. She finally reached it and inserted the magic key card that would start the plush car, giving her access to the inner sanctum of Inferno. Which, she was beginning to think, had been named appropriately since this company really might be the pits of hell.

The doors swished closed and she shut her eyes. She was the toughest person she knew. She had survived an attack at university that had nearly ended in her being raped and the bullying that had resulted when she'd tried to prosecute the boy involved—the son of Starlight, Kentucky's leading family. One grouchy, narcissistic CEO would not stop her from reaching her dream of being somebody. Somebody so important that the people back in Starlight would see that despite all their attempts to break her, she had succeeded.

They had failed.

And Tucker Engle wouldn't break her either.

The elevator bell pinged. The doors opened again. Like Dorothy entering Oz, she stepped out, glancing around in awe. Contrasting the slick, ultramodern red, orange and yellow "fire" theme of the public areas, this space was superconservative. Ceiling-high cherrywood bookcases lined the walls. The antique desk and chair could have been in a museum. Oriental rugs sat on luxurious hardwood floors.

"Don't just stand there! Come in!"

She pivoted around, following the sound of Tucker Engle's voice. He stood in a huge office behind the one she had entered. A cherrywood conference table sat on one side, a comfy brown leather sofa and recliner grouping filled the other. A desk and chair fronted a wall of windows at the back of the room. The view of the New York skyline took her breath away.

She walked to the desk she suspected was hers, removed her jacket and dropped it and her backpack to the chair. Then she gingerly made her way to the grand office.

Standing behind the carved desk, Tucker Engle removed his black suit coat and carried it to a hidden closet. His back to her, he slid it onto a hanger, and her gaze fell to his butt. Perfect butt. His trousers were cut with such precision that they all but caressed him. His simple white shirt outlined a swimmer's back. She could virtually see the ripple of his muscles through the silky fabric. If he didn't do laps in a pool every day, he did something.

She swallowed just as he turned.

"What?"

She swallowed again. Add what appeared to be a perfect body to his dark hair and chiseled features, and he had to be one of the most handsome men on the planet. And he'd just caught her staring at him.

"Nothing."

"Good. Because we have lots to do." He sat and motioned her to one of the two captain's chairs in front of his desk. "Anything you hear in this office is confidential."

She bit her tongue to stop the *duh* that wanted to escape. Not only was that immature, but she had to work with this guy. For weeks...maybe months!

"I'll need more than a dumbfounded look, Miss Prentiss. I'll need a verbal yes."

"Yes. I know about confidentiality. I took ethics classes."

He leaned back. His shirt stretched across his muscular chest. "Lots of people take ethics classes. Not everybody has ethics."

Her eyes narrowed. After two years of being called a liar—a girl who "claimed" she was attacked, most likely in the hope of extorting money—she hated having her integrity questioned. Fury surged through her, but she stopped it. Anger had never gotten her anywhere. A cool head and resolve had.

"I have ethics and I'll keep your secrets."

"Great. Then let's start by filling you in on my latest project. It's the reason I couldn't muddle through the next few weeks with the help of only secretarial support staff."

"Mrs. Martin said you wouldn't tell me your project. That you'd give me assignments piecemeal so I wouldn't be able to guess what you were doing."

"Mrs. Martin is ill informed."

"Maybe you should correct that impression."

His eyebrows rose. "Maybe you should remember with whom you're speaking. You don't get to tell me what to do. Or even make suggestions. Your only job is to perform the tasks I give you."

Embarrassment flooded her. Damn her defense mechanisms for clicking in. She might be proud of the confidence and courage she'd developed to deal with the bullies who'd pushed her around after Cord Dawson attacked her, but Tucker Engle wasn't pushing her around. He was her boss. He was supposed to give her orders.

"Are we clear?"

She didn't hesitate. "Yes."

"Good." He rose, came around to the front of the desk and rifled through some files sitting in the corner. "Constanzo Bartulocci is looking to retire. Do you know who he is?"

"No." The spicy scent of his aftershave drifted to her and her gaze ambled along his torso, down the neat crease of his obviously expensive trousers to his shiny, shiny shoes. If this guy hadn't grown up with money, somebody, somewhere had taught him how to dress. "I don't know who Constanzo Bartulocci is."

"Of course you don't. The über-rich have ways of keeping themselves out of the limelight."

Well, that explained why she hadn't found much about Tucker Engle on the internet.

He located the file he was looking for and returned to his chair. "He never married and he has no children. But he has two nephews and a niece, all three of whom claim to speak for him. Our first job is to weed through the baloney and see who really does know his plans. Our second is to get that person to give us the inside scoop so I know exactly what to offer him for his entire operation."

"You're going to buy a whole conglomerate?"

"Not your place to question, remember?"

"Yes. Sorry." She drew in a breath. How was she going to deal with this guy? Rich, successful and good-looking were bad enough. But she wasn't accustomed to corralling her tongue. Sometimes she even prided herself on being sassy—never letting anybody push her around, condescend to her, make her feel less than.

It would be a long eight weeks if she didn't soon figure out how to keep her place. That is, if he didn't fire her for insubordination.

He handed a file across the desk to her. "Your first assignment is to check the financial reports and records of all of our Bartuloccis."

She glanced up into his bright green eyes and her stomach fluttered. The assignment was pretty much what she'd expected to be doing in the accounting department. So part of the flutter was relief. But the other half came from those striking emerald eyes. He really was one gorgeous guy.

One gorgeous, *difficult* guy, she quickly reminded herself. The difficult canceled out the handsome. And even if it didn't, she'd gone this route before. Cord Dawson had been rich and smart. And in the end, he'd attacked her, nearly raped her. No matter how gorgeous, she wanted nothing to do with another rich guy. She wasn't in their league. Didn't know how to play in their world. It was a lesson she'd never forget.

Taking the file, she rose. "Okay."

He returned his attention to the papers on his desk. "Shut the door on your way out."

She gladly left his office. Closing the door behind her, she squeezed her eyes shut in misery. Even if she learned to hold her tongue, it would be a long eight weeks.

Tucker Engle picked up the employment application, college transcripts, private investigator's report and reference letters HR had sent on Olivia Prentiss. He'd reviewed it all before he'd chosen her, of course, but after meeting her, he needed to be reminded why she'd been his choice to stand in for Betsy.

Excellent grades.

Reference letters that sang her praises as if she were the next Queen of England.

A Facebook profile without pictures of cats—always a plus.

A Twitter account that barely got used. So she wasn't a talker, someone who might inadvertently spill secrets.

Private investigator's report that showed only one incident that had happened her second year at university. A kid from Starlight had sued her for slander. But he'd later dropped the suit. Tucker suspected it was one of those young-love, he-said–she-said things.

Otherwise, she came from a normal blue-collar family in Middle America. Which, he grudgingly admitted, explained why she didn't understand that working directly with him was a coup, not a punishment. God knows, he would have loved someone to give him this kind of opportunity when he'd been through school and starting out in the work world. But after years of moving from home to home as a foster child, he knew it wasn't wise to get close to people he could lose. So, there had been no one to so much as offer him a word of advice when he'd finally started his career. Still, he'd been okay. He'd worked his way to the top—the same way the professors who'd written Olivia's reference letters said she wanted to. Actually, she was a lot like him. Bright. Ambitious.

Unfortunately, she was a little prettier than he'd

expected with her long strawberry blonde hair and her big blue eyes. But he would never get involved with a coworker. Plus, he didn't get involved with women just because they were pretty. He liked his dates to have some class, some charisma and a lot of knowledge. Etiquette and protocol could be taught. And there might be charisma lurking behind Olivia Prentiss's quirkiness. But knowledge? The ability to chat with his peers at a cocktail party or gallery opening? She wouldn't come by that for years. Thus, she did not appeal to him.

Luckily, he hadn't chosen her to be a date. He'd chosen her to write reports, change reports, analyze reports. Her high marks in her accounting classes indicated she could probably do anything he needed to have done.

Satisfied, he made two conference calls. Just as he disconnected the second, his door opened.

"I'm sorry—"

Temper rumbled through him. It was one thing to be clueless about the etiquette of an executive office, to need some experience. It was another to be rude and open a door without knocking. "What are you doing?"

"I don't know how to operate the space shuttle's worth of computer equipment you refer to as a phone, and a call—"

He sighed. "You're supposed to screen calls. I don't talk to just anybody who phones. Go find out who it is. Take their number. I'll decide if I'm calling back."

Her mouth thinned. Her pretty blue eyes filled with storm clouds.

Fine. He didn't like wimps. But he also didn't like interruptions. And there was no better way for an assistant to learn that than by having to go back to her desk and apologize to a caller.

"It isn't a caller. At least not a call for you. The security guard in the lobby is on the line. You have a guest."

"Same instructions. I don't see people who just drop in. Call the lobby, tell them to get the person's name and if I want to I will call him back and schedule an appointment."

"Okay. I guess that means you don't want to see Maria Bartulocci."

His head snapped up. "What?"

"Maria Bartulocci is here. She wants to know if you have time for her. I guess the über-rich don't just know how to keep themselves out of the limelight. They also drop in unexpectedly."

He replaced the receiver of his phone. "Tell them to send her up. Then get a notebook. I want you to sit in and take notes."

She nodded and raced back to her desk.

Missing experienced, polite, sophisticated Betsy, Tucker ran his fingers through his hair. Two minutes later the elevator bell rang. He listened as Olivia greeted Maria and sighed with relief when she was nothing but polite and efficient.

Thick cloying perfume reached him long before dark-haired, dark-eyed Maria did. Tall and regal, educated at Harvard, and well-versed in art and music, Maria was exactly the kind of woman Tucker liked to be seen with. Arm candy with a brain.

"Tucker, how sweet of you to make time for me."

Vivi almost gagged. Holy cow on the cologne, but calling Tucker Engle sweet? This woman obviously wanted something.

"I'm sorry for the wait." He glanced at Olivia, then smiled at Maria. "A little miscommunication with my assistant."

Vivi shook off the insult of that. He hadn't told her any of his preferences, especially not about calls. But he probably assumed she knew those kinds of things, which meant she'd have another assignment that night. Not only did she have to figure out how to stifle her tongue, but she'd have to call her mom, a lifelong administrative assistant, to learn a bit about working for the top banana of a company.

"I'm thrilled you decided to drop in on us." Tucker seated Maria with him on the sofa and motioned for Vivi to sit on the chair beside it.

She opened her notebook.

Maria smiled at her. "No need to record our conversation, darling."

"Miss Prentiss isn't going to record our conversation, just the salient points."

Laughing, she patted Tucker's knee. "Is your memory that bad, Tucker?"

He slid his arm across the sofa, and nearly around Maria. "There are three of you. I'm going to talk with all of you and compare stories."

Her lips turned down into a pretty pout. "Really? You don't trust me?"

He chuckled. "A man doesn't get to where I am without having fail-safe mechanisms in place. Miss Prentiss is one of them."

Maria's gaze crawled over to her.

She took in Vivi's khaki trousers and simple white blouse. Then the long strawberry blonde hair Vivi had put into a ponytail that hung over her shoulder.

"I see."

A flush crept up Vivi's neck to her cheeks. As if the condescending appraisal wasn't bad enough, Maria Bartulocci's tone dripped with disapproval.

Memories of walking down the street, being pointed at, whispered about and called names rushed through her. It had been a long time since she'd remembered that, but it had also been a while since she'd been with someone who so clearly disliked her.

Still, those bullies had nothing to do with her

job, so she ignored the feelings, the memories. She'd learned lots of coping skills in the three years that had passed, and it would take more than a crappy look from a snotty socialite to drag her down.

Tucker said, "Rumor has it your uncle is considering retiring."

"That's not a rumor. It's true."

"Has he set a date?"

"More like a time frame. Next spring." Maria rose. "Take me to lunch and I'll tell you about your competition."

Tucker followed suit, rising to stand beside her. "I know my competition."

"Such a smart man," Maria purred, stepping up to him and running her hand down his tie. "Let's leave the little one behind and get ourselves a drink." She flicked her gaze at Vivi with a laugh. "Really, Tucker, where did you find this one? And why don't you pay her enough to buy decent clothes?"

Vivi's mouth fell open. Seriously? A stinky debutante who was throwing herself at a man had the audacity to criticize *her* clothes?

Tucker caught Maria's hand and led her to the elevator, leaving Vivi behind without a backward glance or even a nod toward telling her how long he'd be gone or how he could be reached in an emergency.

"I don't care what my employees look like. They only have to be able to do their jobs."

The elevator door opened. "I know, but seriously. Did you get a look at her?"

She heard Tucker's voice, but couldn't make out what he said or Maria's reply. The door closed on his laugh.

Vivi glanced down at herself. These were her best trousers, her best blouse. And even she knew she looked like a street waif.

She might have coping mechanisms, but she couldn't argue the truth. She didn't belong here.

CHAPTER TWO

HUMILIATION AND DISAPPOINTMENT followed Vivi
out of the city and up the stairs to the two-bed-
room apartment she shared with her university
friends Laura Beth Matthews and Eloise Vaughn.
Because she and the Grim Reaper had worked
late, she knew her roommates would have already
eaten supper. The scent of spaghetti permeated
the darkly paneled walls of the hall to their third-
floor walkup. But she didn't care. She was too
tired to eat.

Short, sweet, brunette Laura Beth gasped as
Vivi entered the apartment. "You look like hell."

"Thanks." She walked to the refrigerator, which
was only ten feet away from the sofa in their tiny,
open-floor-plan living space, and pulled out a bottle of water.

Eloise, a tall blonde beauty whose wealthy parents had spoiled her rotten, laughed. "First day of
accounting not fun?"

"I'm not in Accounting."

Laura Beth patted the couch cushion beside her and motioned for Vivi to sit. "What happened?"

"Tucker Engle's assistant was in an accident and no one else will work with him. So I have to be his assistant for about eight weeks. But that's all I can tell you because "the" Tucker Engle might share secrets with me, so I'm not allowed to talk to anyone about anything that goes on in his office. Otherwise, I think it's an ethics violation."

Eloise and Laura Beth just stared at her.

Vivi squeezed her eyes shut in misery. "I'm sorry for babbling. I'm tired."

"You're freaking out," Eloise corrected.

"You would be, too, if you spent twelve hours working with a guy you didn't like, who has visitors who are obnoxious."

"You didn't punch anybody did you?"

Vivi took a long drink of water. "No, but I was tempted."

"Are you going to tell us details or are you going to make us guess?"

"I already told you I can't reveal anything that goes on in that office. Confidentiality and all that. But I will say this—I haven't been treated so rudely in three years."

Eloise and Laura Beth exchanged a look. "Bad things happened to you three years ago."

"Exactly."

Laura Beth caught her hand. "Maybe you shouldn't have taken the assignment."

"I didn't have a choice."

"So you have to work with a guy who reminds you of the worst time in your life?" Eloise sucked in a breath. "At least tell me he doesn't look like Cord."

"No and he doesn't act like him either." Cord had always been the life of everybody's party. Grouchy Tucker Engle barely smiled. "But his one visitor today was exactly like Cord's mom… Cordelia Dawson. The woman who thinks her son does no wrong."

"You mean the woman who defended the kid who got you drunk and then attacked you. He would have raped you if you hadn't gotten away."

Vivi froze. They'd talked about this before, but never had Eloise been so blunt, so casual. Laura Beth shot her a warning look.

"Well, I'm sorry, but I think it's better for her to talk about it than to let it fester." She patted Vivi's hand. "Right?"

"Actually, yes." Before that morning, she hadn't thought about being attacked in at least a year. All because she had friends who believed her. Talking, finding people who didn't merely believe her but who'd hurt with her until the hurt was gone, had made her whole.

But she was in the big city now, not in Starlight, Kentucky, at their tiny university. She had to make this job work. "I can tolerate Tucker Engle and his obnoxious guests for eight or so weeks. In fact, I'll do more than tolerate them. I'll be the best damned assistant he's ever had. Then when his real assistant returns I'll go to Accounting where I belong."

Eloise said, "That's the spirit."

Laura Beth patted her hand. "How about if I reheat the leftover spaghetti?"

"No thanks." Vivi rose from the sofa. "I'm exhausted. I think I'll just go to bed."

"Are you sure you're okay?"

"I'm fine. My past is behind me." She forced a smile. "Plus, if tomorrow's anything like today, I'll need all the rest I can get."

After washing her face and changing into pajamas, she crawled into her twin bed beside Laura Beth's, pulled out her cell phone and hit speed dial.

"Hey, Mom."

"Vivi? What time is it?"

"It's around ten. Did I wake you?"

"No, but if I don't get out of bed, I'll wake your father." There was a quiet pause and the click of the closing of her mom's bedroom door. "So what's up? How was your first day at Inferno?"

"Awful. I'm not working in Accounting. I'm the assistant to the CEO."

"Oh! That's exciting!"

Unexpected relief unknotted the tight muscles

of her shoulders. If her mom thought this was exciting, then maybe it was. "Really? I should be happy?"

"You're working with the guy at the top. You should be taking advantage of the opportunity to make a good impression."

"He's kind of a grouch."

"Most older men are."

"Actually, he's not older."

"He isn't?"

"He's kind of young."

Worry filled her mom's voice. "How young?"

"Thirty-ish."

"Thirty-ish? And he's a CEO?"

"He's the *owner* of the company. Which is why he's so bossy. I read online that some of his employees call him the Grim Reaper."

There was a silence. Then her mom said, "I don't like this."

Drat. She should have realized her overprotective mother would be suspicious of any man under fifty. Since her episode with Cord, her parents distrusted every man who looked at her twice. Which was part of the reason she'd moved to New York. She needed some space.

"I'm fine. I'm working for him, not dating him. Plus, his assistant will be back in a few weeks."

"A lot can happen in a few weeks."

"Including that I could prove myself to him like you said I should."

"I don't know, Vivi. I suddenly got really bad vibes about this guy."

"They're the wrong kind of vibes. Mr. Engle has zero interest in me. And all I want is to be able to do this job."

Her mom grudgingly mumbled, "You should be fine. Your grades were great."

"I know I can handle the work. I just need to know some of the etiquette."

Loraina filled her in on a few tips for answering the phone and not speaking unless asked a direct question, but she finished her remarks with, "You be careful with this guy."

As that warning came out of her mother's mouth she winced, realizing what was coming next.

"Your dad and I didn't want you moving to the city. If you could be attacked in a small town by someone you'd known since high school…how the devil can you trust yourself to eight million strangers?"

"I'll be fine, Mom."

"It's just that we worry."

"I know. But trust me. This guy isn't even slightly attracted to me."

Her mother huffed out a breath. "You think. But you're a pretty blonde—"

"Who doesn't have the right clothes or makeup or manners to attract a guy like him." She laughed, remembering the way he liked stinky Maria purring up to him. "Seriously, Mom. I'm perfectly safe with him."

They ended the call, and she settled down on her pillow. Exhausted, she immediately fell asleep and didn't stir until her alarm woke her the next morning.

She showered, headed for her closet and stared at her clothes. She had three pairs of taupe, tan or beige trousers, one pair of dark brown, one pair of gray and one pair of black, as well as seven or eight mix-and-match tops and two summer sundresses that she saved for "good."

Her gaze rolled to her bedroom door. Across the hall was the queen of clothes. Eloise had everything from business suits to ball gowns. They were the same size. She could borrow a nice dress or a fancy blouse and probably fit better into Tucker Engle's world—

No, damn it. She refused to let some condescending socialite bully her into trying to be somebody she wasn't. She was a simple girl. Someone who wanted to prove herself based on her skills and abilities, not her looks. And after her mother's reminder that she should take advantage of this time to prove herself, she'd decided that's how she'd endure these eight weeks. She'd prove herself with her work. Not dress like somebody she wasn't.

When the elevator door outside Tucker's office door opened, he glanced up and saw Olivia Prentiss entering. Today she wore gray trousers with a gray blazer and some kind of clunky sandals. He stifled a laugh. After the way Maria had treated her, he'd wondered if she'd change the way she dressed. He gave her credit for not buckling under to Maria's insults. In fact, he gave her points for that. He hadn't hired her to be pretty or fashionable. They had work to do.

He hung up his phone and walked to the outer office. "Good morning, Miss Prentiss."

She slid her worn backpack to her chair. "Good morning."

Her soft voice told him she didn't want to be here. If she stayed this unhappy, it was going to be a long eight weeks.

He headed for his desk. "We have a busy day today."

She followed him. "Should I get a notebook?"

"No." He paused for a second then made up his mind. Working for him had its boring elements. But he also did some fun things. Maybe if he took her to his signing that morning, she'd see the value of being his assistant. "I need you to study certain files before we go to a meeting."

"We're going out?"

He fell to his chair. "Yes. I'm signing papers this morning to buy a controlling interest in a startup."

Her eyes lit. "Really?"

A zing of pleasure ricocheted through him. He wasn't the kind of guy who needed his employees to be daft with joy all the time. But he did love enthusiasm. And he had made her smile. Which was probably the reason for the zing. Her whole beautiful face lit when she smiled.

"I don't want any snags. So, just in case, I want you and Betsy's laptop with me."

"What am I supposed to do?"

"If there's a question or a problem and I need information, you must be able to find the document and the information in the document."

"From the laptop?"

"Yes." He leaned back in his chair. "I don't keep my files in the company network. It's all in that laptop or my personal internet storage. Betsy had a very simple filing system. You should be able to figure it out quickly. Everything is in a folder called Jason. There will be subfolders under that with names like Legal Documents, Agreement, Financials, Personal. Peruse everything. Get familiar enough that you can find what I need when I need it."

"Sounds simple enough."

"As I said, I don't think there will be a problem. The agreements are already written and preliminarily approved. But just in case."

She nodded and left the room. He stared after her. Her pretty pink top outlined a slim torso. The gray trousers hugged a shapely bottom. Today her long hair cascaded down her back, a shiny strawberry blonde waterfall.

Even dressed like an office worker, she was a knockout. But something was definitely off about this woman. He understood that with her blue-collar background she wasn't quite as classy as most of the women he knew. But that wasn't it. There was something more. She was too cautious.

Shaking his head, he went back to his call list. As long as she did her work, whatever was wrong with her wasn't any of his business.

Vivi spent the next hour skimming files, agreements, financial reports.

A little after ten, Tucker came out of his office, carrying a briefcase. "My car is waiting."

Anticipation stole through her. She probably should have been embarrassed to be so thrilled, but Tucker Engle made superstars out of upstarts, and she would be at one of his agreement signings. She would see what he said, how he behaved. If nothing else, she would see a sharp, savvy guy in action.

They rode down in the private elevator in silence. With the strap of the laptop case over her shoulder and standing straight as an arrow in her gray pants and blazer, she felt like an executive.

The elevator door opened and she followed Tucker Engle to the revolving door and the waiting black limo. He motioned her in first and she slid across the plush leather seat. He sat beside her.

Her blood virtually hummed with joy, but a

knot of fear shadowed it. She'd found the files, familiarized herself with the agreements, the background financials and the sub-agreements over things like whose name would be where as well as the side perks given to the two founders of Jason Jones, a search engine that did simple background checks for real people. She was as ready as she'd ever be.

"Jason Jones is an interesting concept."

Vivi couldn't believe she'd actually spoken, but her excitement had gotten the better of her. And now Tucker Engle would reprimand her.

But he surprised her by chuckling. "When I heard about it, I couldn't believe I hadn't thought of it myself."

"You think you should have come up with it?"

He shrugged. "I would have liked to have thought of it." He peeked at her. "But the best inventions come from ordinary people."

"Really?"

"Yes. People with problems get frustrated looking for answers and sometimes invent or create something with universal appeal."

She nodded.

"Take our startup for instance. Jason Jones is the code name for a private investigator who followed the ex-girlfriend of one of the founders, watching her until he found sufficient evidence to have her convicted of stalking."

She gasped. "One of the founders was stalked?"

"The woman nearly ruined Ricky's life until he realized he had to be proactive and hire a private investigator. The fees were exorbitant. Ricky knew he could have avoided the whole mess if he'd been able to search her on the internet *before* he asked her out."

"But he could have done that."

"No. He could have done a search but not necessarily gotten access to the information that would have saved him. He investigated the systems and Elias Greene wrote the programs. Now innocent men and women everywhere will be able to know a prospective date's *complete* history for fifty bucks and the click of a few keys."

"Amazing."

"Which is exactly why with my help the company will eventually be worth about a hundred million dollars."

The limo rolled to a stop in front of a shiny glass-and-chrome building. They rode to the penthouse in another private elevator, which opened onto a living room. Electric-blue chairs angled beside a black leather-and-chrome sofa, which sat on a modern print rug. A wet bar took up the entire left wall. Huge windows at the back of the room let in the June sunshine as they displayed another fantastic view of the New York City skyline.

Olivia's breath stuttered. She couldn't believe she was here. Not just in a fantastic city, but part of a huge financial deal. Maybe working with Tucker Engle wouldn't be so bad after all?

Two men bounced off the sofa and raced to greet Tucker.

"Hey, Tuck." The first one—a guy who was a lot older than she'd expected, extended his hand. "Big day for us."

"A big day for all of us," Tucker agreed. He motioned to Vivi. "My assistant, Miss Prentiss."

He shook her hand. "I'm Rick Langley." With black hair and silky brown eyes, he was gorgeous. She could understand how he'd meet a woman who wouldn't want to let him go. "The guy with the good fortune to be stalked."

She laughed.

"And I'm Elias Greene."

Vivi shook his hand, surprised when he gave an extra squeeze before releasing her.

Rick bounded to the bar. "Do you want a drink while we wait for our perpetually late lawyers?"

"Miss Prentiss and I are good." He turned to Vivi. "Unless you'd like a water?"

She smiled her appreciation. In one easy sentence, he'd gotten her out of a potentially uncomfortable situation. He really, really wasn't so bad.

She faced Ricky. "Water would be great, thanks. I'd also love a place to set up the laptop."

Elias raced over and took the laptop from her hands. "We're using the dining table as our conference table."

"Sounds great."

Tucker directed her to follow Elias to the table. When she reached it, he pulled out her chair. Ricky handed her a bottle of water as Elias sat beside her.

"So where are you from?"

She cleared her throat. "Kentucky."

"No kidding?" Elias smiled broadly. "Are you a farm girl or something?"

She laughed. "No. I grew up in a small town."

"I'd love to hear about small-town life, if you'd like to have dinner.... Maybe tonight?"

She stared at him. He was serious? Asking her out in front of her boss? But, worse, he was a stranger. And he was asking her out—

She hadn't been out with anyone since Cord.

Heat filled her. She wasn't freakishly afraid of men or dating. After the attack, she'd simply focused on getting her degree. She'd also become selective—too selective to go out with a guy she didn't know.

She drew in a slow breath. "I'm sorry but I don't date people I don't know."

Ricky laughed. "You could always run him through Jason Jones."

She laughed, too, though Elias's proximity suddenly shot shivers of fear through her. Giving him the benefit of the doubt, she chalked his enthusiasm up to excitement over the big, big deal represented by the agreement he was about to sign.

But that didn't make his nearness any less over-whelming.

She rose. "Could you direct me to the powder room?"

Elias popped off his chair. "Sure. It's right back along this hall."

Her nerves went on red alert as they walked down a long dark corridor. A memory flashed. *Cord leading her down a dark hall. Her giggling. Him forcing her into a room. Her fighting to get away and eventually freeing herself. But she'd lost a shoe and her blouse was torn—*

Oh, God. This was bad. She'd put all this be-hind her. Why was it coming back to her now?

In the half bath, she took a few slow breaths. In the quiet, she realized Elias reminded her of Cord. Not looks wise, but personality-wise. A little too pushy. A little too sure of himself.

That's why she wasn't going back out there until the lawyers arrived.

She washed her hands, combed her fingers through her hair and realized she wouldn't hear the attorneys arriving. Nice as he was being on this trip, even Tucker Engle would have his limits. He would be angry with her if she wasn't around when they came.

With a deep breath, she left the bathroom and returned to the main room as the elevator door opened and three gray-suited men stepped out.

Relief stole through her and she quickly made her way to her chair and her laptop.

Laptop! She'd left the laptop containing all of Tucker Engle's business information—information he wouldn't even put on his own company network—unattended.

He was going to kill her.

Tucker watched Olivia with something akin to pride as she not only got herself away from Elias, but also stayed as silent as a church mouse through the entire signing. No smart remarks. No unwanted questions. Just a nice, quiet assistant.

When the papers were signed and after they'd toasted with champagne, which he noticed Olivia refused, they headed for the limo.

As the car wove into traffic, he couldn't stop the compliment that rose up in him. "You did very well in there, Miss Prentiss."

"I did nothing."

"That was your job. You were there in case we needed you. Since we didn't, remaining silent was your only job."

She rubbed her hand down her thigh. "I…um… left the laptop unattended."

"If I remember correctly, you needed to get away from Elias." The memory of Elias ogling her sent a wave of dislike through him, but she'd handled him, and in such a way that there had been no scene and no resultant bad feelings. "And I was in the room. No harm done."

"Really?"

The anxiety in her voice again struck that nerve that told him something about this woman was off or wrong. For a second he toyed with asking her. After all, if she were someone he wanted to do business with he wouldn't hesitate. He always needed to know everything about his partners. But this wasn't a potential business partner. Olivia Prentiss was a temporary assistant. A young, single woman. Did he really want to risk hearing about her bad weekend or latest breakup?

No.

He picked pretend lint off his black trousers. "As I said, you did very well in there."

"Thanks."

She hazarded a glance at him and gave him a shy smile. His instincts hopped again. Trapped by her pretty blue eyes, he sat frozen as the urge to smile back plucked at the corners of his mouth and an unexpected desire to flirt with her rose up in him.

Fortunately, that brought him to his senses. She was a pretty girl and like any normal man, he was attracted to her. But she was an employee. A struggling working girl who shouldn't have to worry about her boss hitting on her.

This "attraction" he felt was purely sexual. The normal reaction of a man to a very pretty woman. Not a big deal. And certainly not something he'd pursue.

* * *

The limo pulled up outside the office building. Tucker exited first and offered his hand to Olivia to help her out.

She took it instinctively, then was sorry she had. Little sparks of electricity spiked up her arm.

Confusion rattled through her. She had been pleased that he'd treated her normally during the limo ride to the signing and again as they drove back to the office. But what she felt right now wasn't boss-employee goodwill. These sparks were attraction.

Really? After Elias had just scared the snot out of her? Three years since she'd even been on a date, she picked today to be attracted to someone? Her boss?

But she hadn't really "picked" anything. This feeling was natural, an instinct. And Tucker Engle wasn't anything like Elias. He wasn't sleazy or overly complimentary or all over her the way Elias had been, the way Cord had been the night he'd attacked her. Tucker was mature, savvy, handsome—sophisticated.

Sheesh, no wonder she was attracted to him. Personality-wise he was Cord's polar opposite.

Fortunately, she didn't think he liked her.

So her being attracted to him was irrelevant.

Thank God.

She slid out of the limo and stopped in front of him on the sidewalk. Their gazes caught and held. Her breath slid in then stuttered out as he just stared at her. His smoldering emerald eyes held her captive. Tingles danced along her hand where their palms touched.

Their palms touched!

Good grief! She still had his hand! No wonder he was staring at her.

She dropped it like a hot potato. "Um. Thanks for taking me with you."

He stepped back. "You're welcome." He took another step away. "I have a lunch meeting. Don't expect me back until two."

"Right." Without waiting for him to get into the limo, she turned and scrambled to the revolving door.

She would not be attracted to her boss.

She would not be attracted to her boss.

She would not be attracted to her boss.

That would be about as stupid as the poorest girl in town dating the son of the local rich family.

And she'd never be that stupid again.

CHAPTER THREE

AT NOON THE next day, Olivia called out "I'm going to lunch," grabbed her backpack and hit the button for the elevator. But before the door opened, the phone on her desk rang.

Not wanting to further disturb Tucker, who'd come back from his business meeting the day before quiet and sullen and hadn't spoken two words to her today, she raced to the phone and answered it. "Tucker Engle's office."

"This is Stewart, the lobby security guard. There's a man and woman here who say they're your parents."

Heat flooded her face and her chest tightened. *Her parents?* Oh, Lord! Their overprotectiveness had now reached its legal limit. It was one thing to check up on her. Checking out Tucker Engle was quite another. How could they embarrass her like this?

"Mr. Engle doesn't allow us to send anybody up to his private offices without prior approval and they aren't on the list."

She thanked her lucky stars for that rule. "No. Of course not. I'll be right down."

"Right down where?"

Hearing Tucker immediately behind her, she pressed her hand to her chest to still her thumping heart, hung up the phone and spun to face him.

"Lunch. I'm going downstairs to lunch, remember I told you that?"

"I did hear you say something. But that was before the phone rang." He caught her gaze. "Who was on the phone?"

Manipulating the timing hadn't worked. And she didn't lie, so this was a moment of truth. Literally. "It was Stewart."

Tucker frowned. "Is he sending someone up?"

Heat blossomed on her cheeks. "No. The people in the lobby didn't have prior approval. So I'm going down."

He turned to his office. "Get him back on the phone. I have time today. I can see whoever is down there."

She stood frozen.

When she didn't answer, he stopped and faced her again.

The warmth in her face intensified. "There's no need to call Stewart. He told me who was in the lobby."

His eyebrows rose.

She sucked in a breath. "It's my parents."

"Oh."

Though it pained her, she knew she might as well go the whole way with this. "I have a sneaking feeling they're here to meet you."

"Sneaking feeling?"

"You know. A feeling that just sort of creeps up on you when you don't want it to."

"Ah." He waited a second then said, "You don't want me to meet your parents?"

"No! No!" What else could she say? "That's not it."

"Then have Stewart send them up. If they're here to see the city, I'll give them my driver for the afternoon and they can go to all the sites."

Though that was nice of him, risking one meeting was bad enough. Risking a second when they returned the limo was insanity. They'd ask questions about his background. Want to know his intentions. Read between the lines of everything he said, making sure he wasn't a closet pervert bent on hurting their little girl. Embarrassment and humiliation collided and turned her stomach. She could not let that happen.

"That's way too kind."

He brushed her concern off with a wave of her hand and headed back into his office. "Call Stewart. Send them up."

With no choice but to obey, Olivia did as she was told.

Fortifying herself for the worst, she stood in front of her desk waiting for the elevator ping.

As the doors opened, she didn't see just her mom and dad. Her brother, Billy, and her sister, Cindy, stood beside them. Even before she was off the elevator, her mother reached out for a hug.

As her mother's arms wrapped around her, she closed her eyes. It was really hard to be mad at somebody who loved you so much.

"Hey, guys."

Her mother squeezed her even more tightly.

"I'm fine, Mom."

As her mother released her, her dad caught her up in a bigger hug. "It's just so good to see you."

She laughed. "I've only been gone a month."

As she said the words, Tucker Engle came out of his office. Her brother and sister froze. Her mom spun to face him. Her dad blatantly gave him a once-over.

Tucker smiled. He had this. If there was one thing he was good at, it was people. Let her dad narrow his eyes. He would still win him over.

Tucker held out his hand to shake her dad's. "I'm Tucker Engle. Olivia's boss."

Tall and bald, Olivia's dad looked like a man who labored for a living. His calloused hand confirmed that.

"Mr. Engle, these are my parents, Loraina and Jim Prentiss and my sister, Cindy, and brother, Billy."

Billy also shook his hand. A boy of about sixteen, who appeared to be trying to be a man, he wore jeans and a T-shirt like his dad.

Her sister Cindy looked a year or so younger than Olivia and was nearly as pretty. Both Prentiss daughters had their mom's strawberry blonde hair and blue eyes. Cindy shyly said, "It's nice to meet you."

But her mom didn't say anything. She caught his gaze and held it as if trying to see into his soul.

He'd never had anyone look at him that way before.

Her pretty blue eyes narrowed, her mouth thinned.

Okay. So her mother didn't like him. He could fix that, too. "I've called my limo driver and instructed him to take you anywhere you want to go this afternoon. It'll be much easier to see everything with a driver who knows the city."

Cindy gasped and Billy said, "All right!"

Jim said, "That's very nice of you." He produced some bags with the logo of a popular Chinese restaurant on them. "But we were just about to have lunch. We brought enough for an army and we'd love to have you join us."

Tucker smiled. "Thank you, but I was planning to work through lunch today. I have a meeting across the street at one. I thought I'd pick up something when that's over."

Loraina surprised him by hooking her arm through his. "Oh, now, you can't skip lunch. And we can't eat in front of you! Besides, if you really are giving us your limo for the afternoon, we owe you."

He sought Olivia's gaze and she shrugged, though her red face was the picture of apology.

He'd never had a family, so he could only imagine how embarrassing this was for her. Especially since her mother was already on the way into his office.

"This is perfect." She pointed at the sofa grouping. "We can sit around the coffee table."

It wouldn't be the first time he'd eaten Chinese food at that coffee table. He did some of his best business deals in that quiet, comfortable atmosphere. He'd never, however, eaten breakfast, lunch or dinner with the family of an employee.

Unfortunately, he couldn't figure out a way to refuse them without sounding like he was kicking them out of his office.

Her dad put the Chinese food on the coffee table. Her brother and sister sat on the sofa and began opening the bags, looking for chopsticks.

Olivia caught his arm and pulled him back, away from her family. "I'm sorry. They're just very comfortable people. They think everybody is a new friend."

He drew in a breath. "That's actually a nice philosophy."

"I swear. In twenty minutes they'll be gone."

Okay. He could deal with that. Hell, he could

deal with anything for twenty minutes. "No need to be so embarrassed or so hard on them. I love the food from the restaurant they chose and as your mom said, everybody needs to eat."

She visibly relaxed and nodded, and his instincts jumped again. All along he'd thought there was something about her. Her family reminded him she was new to the city. Maybe even here alone. And if he got comfortable with her family, maybe she would become more comfortable with him?

He took the big chair at the head of things, reached for a carton of sweet-and-sour pork and dished some onto one of the throw-away plates Olivia's mom had handed out.

"So what do you do for a living, Jim?"

"I'm in construction."

"That's wonderful."

Loraina beamed. "He paid for Olivia's schooling by flipping houses."

"Wow." That took hard work and brains, the ability to find a good house and spend only enough on remodeling that you could still make a profit when you sold it. He could see where Olivia got her talent with numbers.

"He'll do the same for Cindy now."

Cindy faced Olivia. "Are we going to get to see your apartment?"

"I don't know. How long are you guys staying?"

Billy said, "Two days. We have to fly back tomorrow night."

Tucker said, "That's a short stay for such a long trip."

All five Prentisses grew quiet. Olivia's face reddened again. And again the sense that there was something he was missing nagged at him.

But Loraina brightened. "Hotels are expensive in this city. We're just happy for the time we get."

Olivia suddenly said, "Who wants an egg roll?"

Her dad and brother immediately shoved their plates at her, but Tucker suspected she'd craftily changed the subject.

When she faced Cindy, and asked, "Are you ready for school?" he was certain of it.

"I may never be totally ready." Cindy grabbed a different carton of the food and dished herself a serving. "Billy made the football team."

Olivia spun to face him. "Oh, my gosh! Shouldn't you be at practice?"

Billy scowled.

Loraina said, "You can miss a practice or two. It's not every day you get to see New York City."

Ignoring Billy's plight, Cindy said, "I was sort of hoping you'd take me shopping."

Olivia laughed gaily. "Me? I can just barely dress myself. If you want expert advice, you need to take Eloise with you."

Jim said, "I don't think there's time for shopping."

Billy said, "You can shop at home."

Loraina agreed. "You get better bargains there anyway. I saw designers on TV the other day showing how to make clothes from your local store look like big-city fashions."

"I don't want them to *look* like big-city fashions. I want them to *be* big-city fashions. Can't we stay another day?"

Billy exploded. "No! I'm missing two practices already! I'm not missing three!"

"You and your precious football."

"You and your precious *clothes!* At least some day football might get me a scholarship. What are clothes going to get you?"

"A boyfriend?"

"You don't need a boyfriend!"

Both parents said that at once and might have made Tucker laugh, except Cindy's next whine started a discussion that had all five Prentisses talking at once. Tucker had been in boardrooms where five people talked at once. He'd been in boardrooms where five people yelled at once. But this discussion—sort of stupid, but very important to the people talking—whipped around him like a tornado. He had absolutely no idea of what to say.

Worse, he didn't think they cared or wanted him to say anything.

A feeling of alienation stole over him, which didn't surprise him. In foster homes, you didn't comment on another kid's life or problems. You weren't really family; you were boarders. He remembered falling asleep trying to imagine himself in a family like this and never quite being able to put himself into the picture. He couldn't put himself in this picture either. Even though he was actually, physically here.

Olivia's laugh penetrated his discomfort and he glanced from the arguing teens to Jim to Loraina who groaned and said things like "Settle down" and "If you don't stop fighting nobody's getting anything."

He peeked at Olivia again. Her pretty face relaxed in her laughter.

Now she was happy and he was the one who felt like an outsider.

Olivia had never been so glad to see an elevator door open and take people away as she was to see her parents and siblings leave Tucker Engle's office. He made good on his promise of his limo for their use that afternoon, but he'd been quiet through their lunch.

"Do you want me to go back to reviewing Bartulocci financials this afternoon?"

"Yes."

He said the word while staring at the elevator that had just taken away her family and his limo driver.

A minute ticked off the clock. Then another. Then another. He just kept staring at that elevator.

"Are you okay?"

"I'm fine."

But Olivia didn't think he was. Normally, he was a tad brisk. Formal. Even with Elias and Ricky from the start-up, two guys who considered him a friend, he'd been formal. She didn't like this sullen side of him. "I want to apologize again for my family."

"Your family is very nice."

She winced. "My brother and sister fight all the time."

He turned away from the elevator and headed to his office. "I've heard that's normal for brothers and sisters."

She scrambled after him. If this mood was the fault of her family, she had to help him get rid of it. "Heard?"

"I don't have any brothers and sisters."

He strode to his desk and bent down to retrieve a briefcase from the floor. He stopped so quickly, bent so quickly and rose so quickly, that Olivia didn't have time to get out of his way. When he stood again, they were mere inches apart.

She caught his gaze. She could smell the vague scent of his aftershave, feel the raw maleness that drifted off him. After being attacked, she hadn't often let herself get close to a man. Especially not someone as far out of her league as the town rich kid had been—as Tucker Engle *was*.

But he was so handsome and she couldn't seem

to step away, or break contact with his beautiful emerald eyes.

When she spoke. her voice was a mere whisper. "You're an only child?"

"You could say that."

Though they were talking about something totally innocent, electricity crackled between them. "You don't know if you're an only child?"

"No." He took a long breath. "I'm a foster child."

"Oh."

He stepped away. "Don't feel sorry for me. I'm fine."

"Yes, of course."

He walked around her and strode to the door. "This meeting shouldn't last more than an hour."

With that he was gone and Olivia let out her breath in a grand whoosh. A foster child? Her heart ripped in two. Not because he wanted her to feel sorry for him, but because he didn't.

CHAPTER FOUR

WHAT THE HELL was that?

Tucker walked through the building lobby, pushed open the revolving door and stepped onto the sidewalk, his heart beating out a weird rhythm and his mouth dry. He'd told Olivia he was a foster child because it would have been odd to keep a secret that was a matter of public record. He'd said it as if it were no big deal, but having her parents in his office, seeing physical proof of how much they loved her, he knew it was. Eating with them brought back memories filled with scars that had felt like open wounds. Then he'd turned and there she'd been, right at his fingertips, close enough to touch, and damned if he hadn't been tempted.

He combed his fingers through his hair and stopped to wait for the traffic light to cross the street. He could still feel the rush of heat that whipped through him, the swell of sharp, sweet desire. He couldn't remember ever being this attracted to a woman—especially one he barely knew. But standing so close had all but made him dizzy, and holding her gaze had sent molten lava careening through him.

The light turned and he hustled across the street and down the sidewalk. He had a meeting with a few bankers who had a sudden case of nerves about the terms of a deal he'd offered to purchase a struggling manufacturing plant. They needed to be coddled. He couldn't be distracted by an attraction that was out of line.

Ridiculous.

So far off base it shouldn't even be acknowledged.

All he wanted from Olivia Prentiss was for her to do her job.

And he needed to do his.

Heading for the building lobby, he went over the terms of the agreement for Echo Manufacturing in his head. He'd crafted this deal with the precision of an artist. He wouldn't change anything. He had to make the bankers see things his way.

After a two-hour meeting spent attempting to alleviate the concerns of stubborn autocrats with no vision, he was crossing the street again. As persuasive and charming as he'd been, they'd ordered him to totally redraw the offer.

Though that made him forget everything that had happened that morning, it did not make him happy. In fact, if fury were a living thing, his temper would be Godzilla.

His head filled with facts and figures, he entered the elevator to his office suite. He was so immersed in his work that when the doors opened he probably would have walked straight through Olivia's office without even a greeting. But as the doors slid apart, the word *gin!* blasted him.

He stopped. There at Olivia's desk, an empty Chinese food carton on his right, a cup of coffee on his left and a deck of cards between him and Olivia, was Constanzo Bartulocci.

Short and round in the tummy, but dressed elegantly in a tailored gray suit, Constanzo grinned at him. "Good afternoon, Tucker."

"Constanzo?" His head spun. First her parents had arrived and reminded him of everything he hadn't had as a child. Then she'd bowled him over with a little close proximity and eye contact. Then bankers had turned him down. And now the owner of the company he wanted to buy was playing gin—with his assistant?

He wasn't sure he could handle any more surprises today.

The Italian jumped off his chair. "*Sì!* It's good to see you!"

As Constanzo enveloped Tucker in a bear hug, Tucker caught Olivia's gaze.

Her face reddened and she mouthed the words, "He was hungry."

Constanzo released him. "Seven hours on a plane. Two hours in traffic to get here. Starvation and boredom were killing me." He gestured to Olivia. "I hope you don't mind that I begged your assistant to share her food with me."

She grimaced. "We did have leftovers."

His assistant had fed one of the richest men in the world cold Chinese food. Where the hell had his office dignity gone? Where was decorum?

"Yes. I see." He smiled at Constanzo. "I'm glad she had time for you."

Constanzo laughed. "I'm sure she had work, but your Vivi, she is generous."

One of Tucker's eyebrows quirked. *Vivi?*

Constanzo waved his arm in the direction of Tucker's office. "Come. Let's talk about these rumors I'm hearing that you want to buy me out."

Excitement obliterated his anger over the Echo deal and the emotions left over from Vivi's parents' visit. If Constanzo was here at his office, eager to talk about his company, it could only be because he'd made the short list of potential buyers. He motioned for Constanzo to walk before him. "Lead the way."

They headed for the door but Constanzo stopped suddenly. "Vivi, you come, too."

Olivia squirmed on her chair. "Oh, I don't think you need me in there."

"Of course, we do." He inclined his head toward the door. "Come."

Tucker's eyes narrowed. He had no idea why Constanzo wanted her in the room, but one didn't argue with a billionaire who wanted to deal. "Sure, *Vivi,* come."

Olivia smiled sheepishly and rose to follow them. Constanzo barreled ahead, but Tucker waited. Before Olivia reached the door, he caught her arm and stopped her just short of hearing distance for Constanzo. *"Vivi?"*

She shrugged. "It's my nickname. If you'd asked, I'd have let you use it, too."

With a roll of his eyes, he walked into his office, slid out of his jacket and sat on the sofa beside Constanzo. Vivi took the chair across from them.

Attempting to return the room to its usual dignity and decorum, Tucker said, "I'm thrilled to have you in town."

"I like New York."

"You should keep a home here."

Constanzo laughed. "I intend to enjoy not traveling when I retire."

Tucker smiled. *This* was the kind of conversation he expected to have with a billionaire legend. Not a discussion about leftover Chinese food. A feeling of normalcy returned, including the urge to pounce.

Still, he wouldn't jump the gun. He'd continue the small talk until Constanzo brought up the subject of his conglomerate again.

"You might try something like staying in Italy for six months and living in New York six months."

He waved a hand and blew out a "pfft" sound. "Retirement is supposed to be about no plans." He stopped, smiled at Olivia, then turned his attention to Tucker. "Maria tells me you want my company."

"Yes, I do."

"I have something I want, too. If you get it for me, I will negotiate exclusively with you for my conglomerate."

Dumbfounded, Tucker fought a wave of shock. "So there wouldn't be a short list? There would just be me?"

"For a year." Constanzo laughed. "Even you have to admit if we can't come to terms in a year, then there is no deal. But we will negotiate fairly because I want to retire next year. You will find me amicable."

Fighting a feeling that this was too good to be true, or that there had to be a big, ugly catch, Tucker asked, "What do you want me to get for you?"

"You and three others expressed interest in my company."

Tucker had figured as much, so he inclined his head.

"I checked all of your financials, then hired a private investigator."

Not surprised by the review of his financials, but a bit put off by the P.I., Tucker said, "To see who could come up with the financing?"

"No. To see who can bring my son home to me."

Tucker narrowed his eyes. This wasn't a catch. It was a trick. "You don't have a son. You never married. You have no children."

Constanzo laughed. "I see you did your homework too."

"We're both smart businessmen. There's no sense pretending we aren't."

Constanzo slapped Tucker's knee. "That's why I like you. You're on top of things."

"Yet somehow or another I missed the fact that you have a child. Either that, or you're trying to trick me."

"No trick. No one knows I have a child. Thirty years ago on a very busy, very hectic day, a girlfriend approached me saying she was pregnant. Believing she only wanted money, I had her removed from my office. She never tried to contact me again."

Tucker sat forward. "And now suddenly you believe this woman's claim, and you want me to find this child you're not even sure exits?"

"Oh, he exists." He glanced over at Olivia. "I've found him. I only need you to bring him home to me."

"Constanzo, I—"

"—Don't usually get involved in personal family problems to do a business deal?" He laughed. "Is that why you took Maria to lunch on Monday and promised to do something about her annoying cousin?"

"That was part of prying for information."

"That was her undercutting her cousins."

Tucker couldn't argue that so he didn't even try.

"Antonio's mother—the girlfriend I spoke of—died when Antonio was a baby." He reached into his pocket, pulled out an envelope and handed it to Tucker. "He's in Italy now, but he grew up in foster care in the U.S."

Tucker's nerve endings puffed out. *Foster care.* The son of one of the richest men in the world had been raised by strangers. Had gone to sleep lonely. And probably grew up resenting the dad who'd abandoned him.

Which was why Constanzo wanted Tucker to be the one to talk to him. Without even knowing Constanzo's son, he understood him.

"Your investigation went a lot further than I would have expected."

"Yes, and you should be glad because until I went back as far as I did, other candidates to buy my company looked more promising."

Tucker said nothing.

Constanzo sighed. "You're the only one of the candidates who will know how to tell my son he has a father."

"You're saying he doesn't know who you are?"

"No. He does not."

"And you don't want me to just drop in and say,

hey, it's your lucky day, your biological father is a billionaire."

He rose. "I don't care what you say. I leave that entirely to your discretion. With the stakes as high as they are I'm sure you won't make a mistake." He turned to Olivia. "Vivi, a pleasure to meet you. I think you will enjoy Italy."

About to rise, Tucker stopped. "You want me to bring Miss Prentiss to Italy?"

He glanced at Tucker. "Why not?"

"Because she's temporary, only standing in for Betsy, and she doesn't know anything."

"This trip has nothing to do with what she knows. You're buying *my* company. Even you don't know the things I'll share if you win the chance to buy my enterprise."

"Even so, she should stay here so that she has access to things I'll need."

"We have the internet in Italy, Tucker." He laughed. "Besides, I now owe her for her hospitality. I pay her back at my home." He grinned at Olivia. "My cook prepares a lasagna that will make you weep."

She laughed.

He faced Tucker again. "I'm hoping to see you at my villa in the next day or two. Particulars are in the envelope. Good luck."

He left the room and though Vivi popped out of her seat, Tucker watched the realization come to her face that it was too late. Constanzo had already reached the elevator. He pressed the button and the door swished open. There was no point in racing out to escort him.

As the elevator door closed behind Constanzo, Tucker ran his hands down his face. Suddenly the Echo deal falling apart meant nothing. He had an opportunity to get Constanzo Bartulocci's entire enterprise. But, to get the chance for exclusive negotiations, he had to integrate Constanzo's son into his life. And he had to take Olivia Prentiss with him. *Had to*. A wealthy man like Constanzo Bartulocci didn't do anything without reason. He might be trying to make it look casual that he'd invited Olivia along, but after a few seconds to let it all sink in, Tucker knew better. There was a reason.

"I'm not exactly sure why Constanzo wants you on this job, but from the fact that he so clearly handpicked me, I'm guessing there's a reason he's insisting I take you." He motioned her back to her chair. "Sit down. Let's see what's going on here." He ripped open the envelope.

"You're doing it? You're going to Italy to explain to an orphan that he has a dad?"

"There was never a doubt." He glanced at her. "He's offering me exclusive negotiations on a multi-billion-dollar conglomerate."

"Because you were a foster child?"

The words rankled. He should have been pleased that for once his status had gotten him something. Instead, he thought of Olivia's mom and dad. Her arguing sister and brother. He wondered what it might be like to grow up surrounded by people who loved you enough that they traveled thousands of miles to see you simply because they missed you.

And got angry with himself. He'd forgotten all this, let it go. One episode with a quirky family shouldn't make him long for things that couldn't be. No one could change the past.

His gaze fell to the documents in the envelope. Pictures of a young man with Constanzo Bartulocci's eyes. A birth certificate that named the baby's father as unknown. But a DNA test that proved Constanzo was the father.

"Well, I'm not sure who his P.I. was but he's thorough."

Vivi rose from her chair and sat beside him so she could see the papers. "Why do you say that?"

He turned to hand the DNA test to her but their gazes caught and those weird feelings swept through him again. The pinpricks of awareness. The warmth of excitement. The swirl of desire. Except this time they came with the knowledge that he was taking her to Italy. They'd spend seven hours alone on a plane, eat every meal together—

But Tucker dismissed those concerns simply by looking away. He might be attracted but he wouldn't pursue it. She was his employee but more than that, she wasn't his type. He liked sexy sophisticates. She was a family girl. Too sweet for him. Or maybe he was just a little too rough for her.

"To get DNA for the test, Constanzo's investigator probably trailed the poor kid until he could get his used cup at a coffee shop or something."

Vivi laughed. "Really? You think that's what he did?"

"He certainly couldn't ask for a lock of his hair."

"Not unless he wanted to get arrested. Or alert Constanzo's son that someone was investigating him. I'm guessing Mr. B. doesn't want his name even mentioned until the road is clear for a congenial meeting."

Tucker sat back on the sofa. She'd brought the situation down to its real bottom line, and quickly enough that Tucker wondered if that was why Constanzo wanted her to go to Italy. She'd probably said something while they were playing cards to make him think she was smart, intuitive, good with people.

And maybe she was. Tucker might understand being a foster child, but she understood being poor. She also knew about family.

"Are you sure you don't mind me going to Italy?"

"Constanzo Bartulocci is one of the richest men in the world. You don't get rich by being stupid or by not understanding people. He sees something in you. Something he thinks I might need. Wouldn't I be a little foolish to refuse his back-handed advice?"

"I guess."

He slid the papers back into the envelope. "Pack tonight. We'll leave tomorrow after work."

She rose. "Okay."

He walked to his desk, dismissing her, but stopped suddenly. "And Miss Prentiss make sure your parents are on board with this trip."

There was no way he'd take her anywhere if big Jim and narrow-eyed Loraina didn't want him to.

CHAPTER FIVE

VIVI CALLED HER parents and made arrangements to meet them at a pizza place by their hotel for dinner. When she dropped the bomb about Italy, her dad went ballistic. Her mom absolutely forbade her from going.

"I'm twenty-two. You can't stop me. Besides, you met him. He's a wealthy man who can have his pick of women. Trust me. He doesn't want the local street waif." Even as she said the words, she knew they were something of a lie. Not a total lie, but kind of close. She didn't know what had happened when Tucker Engle had bent to pick up his briefcase and suddenly they'd been two inches away from each other. But her attraction to him had turned her voice to a whisper and she'd seen the spark of something in his eyes.

Still, he'd ignored it. Pretended it wasn't there. He might find her attractive but he didn't want to. Which meant he wouldn't act on the weird feelings hopping between them, and, technically, that was all her parents were interested in.

"You're a very beautiful woman. You don't think it's odd that you go to work for him one day and three days later he decides to take you across the Atlantic?"

She brightened. "That's just it. He doesn't want me to go. He wants to buy the company of a man named Constanzo Bartulocci. Mr. Bartulocci dropped in today unannounced and gave Mr. Engle the chance to be the sole bidder on his company. But to get the chance to bid, he has to go to Constanzo's estate in Italy."

"With you?"

"Only because Mr. Bartulocci wants me to go, too."

"Why?"

"Because I'm part of Tucker Engle's team. With his regular assistant gone. I'm his go-to girl."

When her parents still looked unconvinced, she sighed. "I am twenty-two years old. I had something really bad happen to me three years ago. I got beyond it. And do you know why? Because if I didn't, if Cord had made me too scared to live, then he didn't just steal my reputation from me. He also stole my life and, frankly, that's something I refuse to give to him."

Her dad tossed his napkin to the table. "You have a point."

Her mother shook her head. "It's just that Tucker Engle is so young."

"Yes, he is young, but he's a very smart guy.

Before you found out how old he was even you told me I could learn from him."

She reached across the worn table of the pizza place and caught her mother's hand. "Don't trust him, Mom. Trust *me*. I need to get out in the world to prove I've recovered."

Twenty minutes later, she was walking home to pack.

The next day she brought her single piece of luggage and a toiletries case to work. Tucker had meetings out of the office all day in preparation for being away, so he had left the limo for her and told her he would meet her at the airstrip.

Traffic kept her on the road until almost seven, filling her with panic. But when she saw the long, sleek jet that stood at the ready, she forgot all about being late and gaped at it in awe. Tucker Engle *owned* that glossy little jet. For all she knew he also owned the airstrip.

He was a former foster kid who at thirty or so now owned a plane. Maybe an airstrip. It was phenomenal.

And she suddenly understood why she was so drawn to him. He'd done what she wanted to do. He hadn't let his past hinder him. He'd gotten beyond it.

Technically, she might not be attracted to him as much as she admired him.

She thanked the driver who assured her he

would see to her luggage, and casually headed for the plane.

A tall, blue-eyed pilot greeted her as she entered. "Good evening, Miss Prentiss."

She smiled. "Good evening."

"The flight is approximately seven hours. Accounting for the time difference, we'll be arriving at Mr. Bartulocci's private airstrip around 7:00 a.m. local time."

"So, you're basically telling me to sleep on the flight?"

"Yes, ma'am." He motioned her toward the roomy six-seat cabin.

Tucker Engle sat at a compact workstation at the very back of the plane. Paperwork had been spread out on the table in front of his seat. Though he said good evening, he barely looked up from his work, confirming that he might be attracted to her but he wasn't interested in her. Her parents had nothing to worry about.

She slid into one of the six butterscotch leather seats and buckled in. The pilots taxied to the runway and the plane took off smoothly.

She reclined her seat, preparing to fall asleep. But soft as it was, without a pillow or a blanket, she couldn't quite get comfortable.

"There are blankets in a cupboard back there."

She sat up and faced him. He angled his thumb toward the back of the plane. "And pillows."

She unbuckled her seat belt and rose. "Thanks."

She walked to the cupboard, but she didn't open it. Her hand hovered over the door knob. "Would you like one?"

"No. I'm working."

She nodded and returned to her seat with a pillow and a blanket. She turned off the light above her, reclined her seat and nestled into her covers.

She closed her eyes and took three long, calming breaths, but they didn't help. She couldn't imagine how someone went from being a foster kid to being a billionaire. She had had help from her parents, but still couldn't live in New York City on her meager salary without roommates. Starting at the bottom, she had absolutely no idea how to climb the ladder from where she was now to where he was now.

And that's what she wanted. To be somebody. So that when she went back to Starlight everybody would see she hadn't needed to fake an attack to extort money from Cord Dawson. She had always had the talent and drive to be successful on her own.

She sat up, swiveled to face him. "So how does somebody go from being a foster child to owning all this?"

He didn't even look up. "Perseverance."

"There's got to be more to it than that."

"There isn't."

"It's not like I wouldn't understand. I'm pretty smart and I really want this. Plus, it's not like anything you'd say would shock me. I had a friend who was a foster child. And I also had some really crappy things happen to me at university."

He knew she had. He remembered she'd been sued for slander. Even though the kid had dropped the suit, she'd probably been terrified.

He twirled his pencil between his fingers. He shouldn't talk. He should keep everything between them strictly professional, but she'd opened the door and curiosity about that "something" about her wouldn't allow him to let the opportunity to ask her a few questions pass. If she wanted to know his secrets, first she'd share hers. "I know about the lawsuit filed against you three years ago."

Her eyes widened. "You do?"

"Like Constanzo, I go the extra mile with people who are going to know my business."

She said nothing, but her face had gone pasty white.

"I understand the kid dropped the suit, but it would still be very difficult to be nineteen and have somebody sue you."

She nodded.

"So what happened?"

"Happened?"

"No twenty-year-old boy files a slander law suit without good reason. So whatever you said, it had to have been a doozy."

Her chin lifted. "I told the truth."

"Then it couldn't have been slander."

"I couldn't prove what I said."

"Oh." He caught Olivia's gaze. "But it was true?"

She nodded.

"Which was probably why he dropped the suit. He didn't want to risk that you'd find a way to prove it."

"Oh, he knew I couldn't."

Curiosity spiked again, and he nearly kept going, so intrigued about her that the work in front of him had lost its appeal. But he suddenly realized he was comfortable, talking about personal things—the kind of things he never talked about with anybody, especially not an employee.

He'd already decided he didn't want to be attracted to her, so what was he doing getting to know her?

"Why don't you try to sleep while I do some work? This trip to Italy is going to cost me a hundred other things if I don't get my ducks in a row now. So no more talking."

"Okay."

She turned around and he forced his attention back to work. Work had made him who he was today. He didn't need conversation. He didn't need family. He needed only to be the best he could be.

Tucker Engle's plane landed at Constanzo Bartulocci's private airstrip in the Italian countryside.

A driver waited by a white limo and they headed for Constanzo's villa.

Vivi stared out the window in awe. A sea of green grass flowed to mountains. The sky was the bluest blue she'd ever seen, hovering over the grassy slopes like a benevolent blue god. "This is gorgeous."

Pulling a document from his briefcase, Tucker said, "Italy's a beautiful country."

She almost asked if he always worked but she knew the answer to that. Of course, he did. Now that he'd told her he'd been a foster child, so many things about him made sense. Just as she saw success as a way to vindicate herself, he probably saw it as a way to prove his value to a world that hadn't wanted him. It was why he'd flown to Italy in a black suit, white dress shirt and black-and-silver striped tie, while she'd worn plain trousers and a yellow shirt. He never stopped. Never relaxed. Everything was work to him.

And she supposed she had her answer for how he'd climbed his way from foster child to billionaire. He worked all the time.

They arrived at Constanzo's country villa and Vivi nearly broke her neck looking around, trying to see everything at once. Trees and shrubbery provided privacy. Lush green grass bordered stone walks that took them to the front door of a stone house that could have been hundreds of years old but had been updated.

"Welcome! Welcome!" Wearing dress pants and a short-sleeved shirt, open at the neck, Constanzo greeted them in the foyer. A colorful tile stairway with a black iron railing led to the second floor. Antique tables along the walls held vases of fresh flowers. Though the house was big, it wasn't the stuffy mansion Vivi had expected a billionaire to live in. Beautiful and colorful, it was also homey.

Constanzo hugged Vivi then Tucker. "My staff is putting your things in your rooms. Would you like time to freshen up?"

Vivi yawned. "Actually, I'd like a nap. I couldn't sleep on the plane." Her brain had been so jumpy she hadn't been able to relax. So she'd pulled her book out of her purse and read for most of the flight.

Constanzo laughed. "Vivi, Vivi. The best way to get accustomed to a new time zone is to pretend your body is already on our time."

"I've been up twenty-four hours! I'll never make it."

Constanzo put his arm around her shoulder. "Of course, you will. It'll be bedtime here before you know it." He led her up the winding staircase. "Take a shower, put on fresh clothes. Something comfortable like jeans and I'll show you around. We'll go to a little café in town for lunch, then come back here for supper."

"Or she could take a nap by the pool while you and I discuss business."

In her tired state, she'd actually forgotten that Tucker was behind them. But she wasn't surprised he wanted to talk details of their deal. He was here to work.

Constanzo laughed. "Before we discuss business, you have a mission."

"Yes, but there are plenty of details we could—"

Constanzo made the "pfft" noise again. "We'll get to the details after I show Vivi around."

For the first time since she'd become Tucker's right-hand girl, she got a tug of assistant responsibility. Now that she understood a little about him and his work ethic, she knew what she had to do. "Actually, I'd rather see the town on a day when I'm rested." She smiled at her host. "Besides I have a feeling I could spend the day exploring your villa and the grounds."

Constanzo waved his hand dramatically. "Then that's what you'll do."

She laughed. Constanzo showed her to a little room decorated lavishly in shades of lavender and white. A June breeze fluttered the sheer white curtains, bringing with it the scent of fresh grass and wild flowers.

"This room is beautiful. Like art."

"Life is art. It's to be enjoyed." Constanzo opened the door on a stunning bathroom with white marble tiles and showed her a closet where her clothes already hung.

"Your staff is fast!"

"They like their jobs and want to keep them."

"So, Tucker and I will leave you to explore. If you need a swimsuit, dial five-one on the phone and explain what you want. We have plenty for guests. And my staff speaks English."

She smiled her thanks and he and Tucker left.

She breathed in the scent of fresh air, something she hadn't smelled since her last visit to Kentucky, and twirled around. She was in Italy! On the estate of a billionaire! She fought the urge to pinch herself and, instead, slipped out of her sandals.

The bed called to her but she agreed with Constanzo that the best way to adjust to her current time zone would be to eat, drink and sleep at the appropriate times. Which meant she had to entertain herself for the next few hours.

After a quick call to the staff, a maid brought her a raspberry-colored one-piece swimsuit in the size she requested. The tags had been trimmed, but she could tell the suit was new.

She showered, shimmied into the tight spandex suit, slid into the cover-up and big straw sunhat the staff had also provided, and grabbed her book before she made her way downstairs. To the right were closed double doors. A formal dining room, complete with crystal chandelier, sat on the left.

A slim hall ran down the middle. She followed the corridor to a huge great room. Floral sofas flanked by crystal lamps dominated the room. Huge double doors provided a view of the pool, its blue water sparkling in the sun.

She walked through the double doors onto a gray stone patio to a row of canvas chaise lounges. Kicking off her shoes, she tossed her book to the chair so she could remove the white lace cover-up.

When she finally had herself settled on the chaise, the June sun warmed her and giddy peace filled her. She was in Italy. *Italy.* She'd ridden a private jet across the Atlantic, driven in a limo, been brought to a villa where maids unpacked her meager belongings and now she lounged by a pool.

After leaving Olivia in her room, Constanzo had shown Tucker to the lavish suite he would be using. He'd suggested Tucker might want a nap or maybe a few minutes to freshen up. But Tucker insisted they use the time to hash out some of the details of the conglomerate acquisition. So Constanzo had led him to a den at the back of the first floor.

A pool table sat in the center of the room. Four big-screen TVs, one for each wall, hung in strategic spots. A bar that looked like an old English pub took up the back corner.

Constanzo immediately strode to the bar. "So what's your pleasure?"

"Details. You're offering me a billion-dollar conglomerate. I'd think the first order of business would be to stipulate how we'll determine market value."

"No! No!" Constanzo laughed. "I meant your drink. You like American bottled beer or what I have on tap?"

Tucker held back a sigh of impatience and politely said, "I'll try what you have on tap."

Constanzo drew two drafts and handed one to Tucker.

"Thanks. So how are we going to determine market value?"

Constanzo pushed a button and a dartboard appeared. "We could use the numbers in my annual statement."

"And disregard what's happened since it was released? How do I know your companies haven't gone down in value?"

He opened a carved box filled with darts that lined both the bottom of the box and its lid, and offered them to Tucker. "Because you've been watching me. You know exactly what I'm worth."

Tucker chuckled. He took a dart, aimed at the board and made a bull's-eye.

"Ah. A real challenge for me today!"

Tucker sighed. "You're not going to talk business, are you?"

"No. You're tired from your trip. It wouldn't be fair."

"Right. Don't try to kid somebody who makes his living knowing when people are lying to him."

"All right. You want to be blunt. We will be blunt. If you can't deliver my son to me, totally understanding my position—that his mother contacted me once, on a busy day, when I was so overwhelmed I barely registered what she said, let alone had brain power to believe it—then you don't get my company."

"So there's no point in talking specifics?"

"Exactly." As he spoke, Constanzo opened the drapes of the den, revealing his shimmering pool. The gray stone outdoor space had furniture groupings that ran the gamut from formal seating areas to casual placement of chaise lounges around the pool.

And on one of the chaise lounges lay a pale woman in a one-piece, pinkish-purple bathing suit. A lock of strawberry blonde hair blew in the slight breeze.

Olivia. *Vivi.* Casual, happy, like-me-as-I-am Vivi. The woman who'd actually drawn him into a personal conversation the night before.

"I worry she'll fall asleep in the sun."

Tucker took a swig of beer. "If she does, she'd better have sunblock."

"She is pale."

She was pale. Trusting. And he'd finally realized that was the thing that drew him about her, even as it annoyed the hell out of him. She wanted to understand, asked a million questions, because she wanted to trust life.

Trust life. As if one could.

He took in her smooth shoulders, her trim tummy. Even being exactly the opposite of what he liked in a woman, she tempted him.

Which was ridiculous. He liked sleek, sophisticates. Not hometown girls.

She shifted on the chaise, onto her side. The hat slid over her face, but the position pushed her breasts precariously high in the brightly colored suit. Her long legs stretched out, bared to him on sand-colored canvas. All right. She was sexy. She might not be sleek or sophisticated, but she was definitely sexy.

"Vivi...she is more than your assistant?"

Tucker swung around. Good God. Now the woman had him staring. "No." He walked over to the bar and grabbed three darts. "I told you, she's really not even my assistant. Betsy, the accountant who generally works with me was in an accident. Vivi—" Oh, Lord. Had he just used her nickname? "Is a temp."

He laughed. "I see."

"She probably won't be with me the next time we meet. But you'll like Betsy. She's incredibly competent."

And he was counting the days until she finished rehab and returned to the office. He didn't want a sexy assistant. He didn't want to wonder about the slander suit filed against her. He wanted Betsy back so his life could return to normal.

Still, every time Constanzo took his turn at the dart board, Tucker's gaze drifted out to the pool.

"Drink, Miss?"

The white-coated butler scared Vivi awake and she jumped. She shouldn't be surprised that she'd drifted off to sleep since she hadn't even had so much as a nap on the plane. But she didn't want to sleep. She wanted to adjust to her new time zone.

"Sorry for jumping."

He smiled benignly. "It's quite all right."

She wasn't in the mood for a drink, but a little caffeine might give her some energy. "Do you have iced tea?"

"Yes, ma'am."

He left as quickly and quietly as he'd arrived, brought her drink and disappeared again. She sipped her tea, then flipped over so she didn't get too burned.

But even before she settled on the chaise, she had the strangest feeling. Like someone was watching her.

She sat up and glanced at the house. The entire back of the first floor of the renovated house looked to be a wall of windows. Because of the framing, she guessed some of the 'windows' were actually double doors. But the angle of the sun made the glass dark. She couldn't see inside.

She adjusted the strap on her suit, smoothed her hands down her legs, unable to shake the feeling of being exposed.

She frowned. Of course, she was exposed. She was outside. Lounging on the patio of a house that had at least one maid, a butler and a driver. There was probably a cook and a gardener, too. Four people could be gawking at her if they wanted to be. But why would they want to?

It was stupid to be paranoid. A better explanation for what she was feeling was guilt that Tucker and Constanzo were working and she wasn't. She hadn't come to Italy to lie about. As it was, Tucker Engle didn't like having her along. Even if the trip had been grueling and she was tired, she had to get to work. Plus, she'd had a nice little nap. She had her brain back.

After gathering her cover-up, she padded to her room, put on her plain trousers and yellow shirt and headed downstairs again.

The house was a maze of corridors and beautifully decorated rooms. She could have stopped in every parlor to examine the furnishings and art she was sure was real, but needing to find Tucker and Constanzo, she kept looking until she found the pair in a den.

Playing darts. Drinking beer.

She shook her head. "You know, I was out by

the pool, feeling bad because I wasn't working, and here's where I find you guys? Playing darts."

Tucker faced her. His suit coat lay across the back of an overstuffed recliner. His white shirt sleeves had been rolled up to his elbows, his black-and-silver striped tie loosened. He looked so casually gorgeous, she swallowed hard.

Her foolish attraction was growing, but at least now she understood why. He'd grown up poor, but he was successful now. Just as she wanted to be. They had common ground. He wasn't just a good-looking guy. He was somebody she wanted to know.

"Vivi, come in! Do you throw?"

Glad for the distraction of Constanzo, she settled herself on the arm of an overstuffed chair beside the pool table. The room wasn't dripping with diamonds or gold the way one might expect a billionaire's house might be. Instead it seemed to exist for Constanzo's comfort. Which, she supposed, was the way a billionaire should live.

"No, I don't throw."

"Your boss is beating me."

She laughed. But Tucker kept his attention focused on the dart game. She hoped he wasn't angry with her. He was the one who had suggested she sit by the pool while he and Constanzo talked. So he *couldn't* be angry with her.

She let her gaze drift around the room but she stopped suddenly when she saw the chaise lounge with the empty iced-tea glass sitting on the table beside it.

Her gazed jerked to Tucker's. This time he didn't look away. His perfect emerald eyes heated. Her breath leached out in a slow hiss. Pinpricks of awareness skittered down her spine. He'd seen her in the bathing suit.

She tried to be Zen about it, because, really, it was a one-piece suit. So what if he'd seen her legs? It meant nothing.

But he didn't let go of her gaze and she couldn't let go of his.

Okay. So it meant something.

He picked up a dart and tossed it toward the board. It landed with a thud that mirrored the thudding of her heart. She didn't want to like another guy who was so far out of her stratosphere... but how did she stop this? Her feelings for him were unexpected. So natural she didn't have any warning they were going to pop up until they did. And his?

She had no idea.

CHAPTER SIX

PLEADING A NEED to get some work done, Tucker left the den shortly after Olivia arrived and she didn't see him again until he entered the dining room for dinner that evening.

As Tucker walked in one door, Constanzo entered from the other side. Concern wrinkled his forehead and turned his mouth into a frown. "I'm so sorry. There's a problem at one of my companies. We are video conferencing in ten minutes. I would tell you that I'll return shortly and join you for dinner, but the problem is significant."

Vivi's heart stuttered. She and Tucker Engle had to eat alone?

Tucker said, "I understand."

She just barely kept herself from groaning. It absolutely looked as if they were eating alone.

"Excellent. You and Vivi enjoy dinner."

He scurried out of the dining room and Tucker faced her.

As always, he wore a dark suit that looked to have been made for him, white silk shirt and silver tie. She wore a light-weight floral dress with thin straps, something she'd bought at the end of the season the year before and paid less than half price for. Her hair hung straight—freshly washed, but just straight. His shiny dark hair had been combed to perfection.

If that wasn't a reminder that they lived in two different worlds she didn't know what was. He'd never make a pass at her and, if he did, she'd never flirt back because they did not belong together. They were too different.

But even before she finished that thought, he loosened his tie and pulled it off then undid the top two buttons of his shirt.

"Good evening, Miss Prentiss."

Oh, Lord. He was dressing down for her. And casually, so he wouldn't embarrass her. It was the sweetest thing, but she reminded herself they weren't a good match. He might be the first guy she was attracted to since Cord, but he wasn't interested in her. He was only being polite. A man who was interested wouldn't call her Miss Prentiss.

"Good evening, Mr. Engle."

He motioned toward a chair and she walked over. He pulled it out and she sat.

Ambling to the seat across the table from hers, he asked, "Do you know what Constanzo's cook prepared?"

"This afternoon he told me she was making a lasagna as lasagna is supposed to be made."

He laughed. "Leave it to him to be melodramatic."

"If it tastes as good as it smells, I think he's allowed a little melodrama."

As servants filled their glasses with water, Olivia struggled to think of something to say. Thick with the protocol of servants and a long row of silverware, the scene reminded her yet again that she and Tucker Engle had nothing in common.

When the servants left, she took a quiet breath and said, "Constanzo beat me in four games of pool this afternoon."

"It was kind of you to entertain him."

"He says it's boring for an old man to sit around his house with nothing to do. He says he should have grandkids and be teaching a little girl how to swim and a little boy how to hustle pretty girls in pool."

He laughed.

Her chest loosened a bit. This wouldn't be so bad. All she had to do was keep talking. "I think he was just distracting me with chitchat so I wouldn't notice how badly he was beating me."

Servants arrived with salad and bread and they dug in. For the next few minutes conversation revolved around how delicious the crusty bread was, then the table grew quiet.

She scoured her brain to think of something to

say and couldn't come up with anything. Seconds ticking off the clock felt like hours, reminding her yet again that she shouldn't be attracted to a man with whom she had nothing in common.

The main course came. At the first bite they groaned in ecstasy and complimented the lasagna, but the conversation stopped again. The longer they were quiet, the more obvious it was that they had nothing to say to each other and that any attraction she felt for him was foolish.

When she finished her dessert, she looked at her watch. Not even nine o'clock.

Across the table, Tucker surreptitiously looked at his watch, too.

For two people with palpable chemistry, they were certainly eager to get away from each other.

Tucker rose from his seat, tossing his napkin to his empty dessert plate. "So how about if you and I play a few games of pool?"

Her head snapped up. "Really?"

"If we go to bed now, we'll be up at four o'clock. Do you want to sit around with nothing to do for hours and hours?"

"I was kind of thinking if we went to bed now I'd sleep for hours and hours."

He laughed. "Are you ready to retire for the night?"

She shrugged. "I don't know. I think your idea of staying up a few more hours might be better."

"Great."

They walked to the den in silence. As she chose her pool stick, Tucker racked the balls. With a nod toward the table, he let her break. She dropped one of the striped balls into the pocket but missed her second shot and Tucker took over. The den filled with the crack of his stick against the balls and the plop, plop, plop of ball after ball falling into a pocket.

In the face of the beating she was taking, she forgot all about the quiet. Why was it she could beat any group of guys in a bar, but not whip the butts of two billionaires?

"Okay. I wasn't quite ready to play. Rack the balls again. This time I won't be so easy."

He laughed. "We'll see."

"Ah, smug, this time around?"

Tucker arranged the balls on the table. "Not smug. I just watched how you play. My technique is better."

"Right."

He motioned to the table as he walked behind the bar to pour himself a draft. "Go ahead. I'll give you the advantage. Break again."

She strolled up to the table, aimed her stick and broke with a resounding crack that echoed around them. Two solid balls dropped. She faced him with a grin. "I have you now."

He leaned against the bar. "What? You think solid is going to be lucky for you?"

"Yes." She walked around the table considering

her next shot. When she found it, she bent across the table to take aim.

But Tucker shook his head. "Your form is all wrong."

"My form is fine."

"No. Look at your stick. It wobbles." He walked behind her and leaned down with her so he could adjust her arm. "See? Isn't that better?"

The feeling of his chest along her back sent waves of awareness flowing from her back to her toes. He stepped away, as if totally oblivious and, shell shocked, she took the shot.

Miraculously, the ball she aimed for fell. She jumped up with a whoop of joy. "I did it!"

He motioned at the table. "Keep going."

She picked a shot and leaned over the table, but again he shook his head

"Your stick still wobbles." Positioning himself over her, he leaned down and straightened her arm. Then he froze.

The room grew quiet.

Warmth radiated from him into her and would have sent a shudder through her if she hadn't ruthlessly stopped it. She turned her head slightly to catch his gaze. His green eyes smoldered.

Oh, boy. This wasn't good.

Tucker stayed frozen. The woman was the softest thing he'd ever touched. Every hormone in his body awakened at the feel of her skin sliding against his. His hand itched to leave her pool stick and cruise along the curve of her waist, to turn her around, so he could kiss her.

The instinct was so strong, so natural that it shook him to his core and brought him back to planet earth. She was an *employee. Smart executives did not kiss employees*.

He stepped away and ambled back to the bar, pretending nothing had happened, confused that he couldn't seem to get himself under control around her.

As he picked up his beer from the bar, Constanzo walked in.

"Great! I see I'm just in time! I'll play the winner."

Olivia took her next shot but missed this time. Without looking at him, she said, "Your shot."

He licked his suddenly dry lips. Okay. That thing between them? He now had confirmation she felt it, too. But he could handle this. *They* could handle this. They'd just pretend it hadn't happened.

He set down his beer, picked up his pool cue and walked to the table. He got two balls in then missed, surprising Olivia who quietly walked up to the table again. She hit the remainder of her balls into the pockets, beating him soundly.

"Looks like you and me, Vivi," Constanzo said, happily rubbing his hands together.

But Olivia yawned. "You and Mr. Engle play. I think it's time for me to go to bed."

He didn't know if she really was tired or trying to get away from him, but he breathed a sigh of relief.

Until Constanzo said, "Tucker will walk you to your room."

The blood froze in his veins. He couldn't walk her to her room! He was unstable around her. Confused. He wanted to be away from her, not walking down a dark corridor with her.

Olivia shook her head. "I'm fine. I know the way."

But Constanzo said, "Vivi, you will not go upstairs alone. Walking a lady to her room is what a gentleman does."

It *was* what a gentleman did and that reminder corralled Tucker's hormones and got him back to reality. He was a gentleman and she was an employee. Worry that he couldn't keep himself in line was ridiculous.

He set his beer glass on the bar. "Nonsense. You're asleep on your feet. I'll walk you to your room."

They said goodnight to Constanzo who racked the balls again. Walking out of the den, Tucker heard the sound of silence left in their wake. Constanzo had put on the soccer game, and there was noise when he broke the balls on the pool table, but just beneath the surface of those sounds was a quiet nothing. And he suddenly understood why Constanzo wanted his son. When he retired, *this* would be his life. Entertaining an occasional visitor or two would fill the void, but mostly he would be alone. He wanted that "nothing" filled with the sound of his child, and maybe, someday, grandchildren.

"Why do you call me Miss Prentiss?"

They'd reached the end of the hall and were heading for the stairway in the front foyer. Focused on Constanzo, he hadn't noticed how far they'd come. He'd also forgotten about his attraction. But the minute she spoke, his body reacted.

Still, she was an employee and he was a gentleman. He motioned for her to precede him up the stairs. "I call you Miss Prentiss because it's your name."

"So is Olivia. Or Vivi." She stopped and peered back at him. "And I have to admit, sometimes it feels a bit weird having to call you Mr. Engle when everybody else is calling you Tucker."

Just what he and his hormones needed, for another of the barriers between them to come tumbling down. "I'm always on a first name basis with people I do business with. You are an employee."

"An employee who has to call you something different from what everybody else calls you."

He should have been annoyed with her impertinence. Instead, he understood. They were two incredibly attracted people who, in any other circumstance, would be getting to know each other, probably pursuing this attraction. But she was an employee. And he was a gentleman.

He repeated it like a mantra in his head as they walked down the hall. When they reached her door, she stopped and faced him.

"Good night, *Tucker*."

Damn it. He almost laughed. She could be such a smart-ass. Worse, he'd liked the sound of his name on her lips. He liked that she was so bold.

"You're a brat."

"No. I just don't appreciate anyone trying to make me feel less than."

Confused, he stepped closer. "You think that's what I'm doing? Trying to make you feel less than me?"

She shrugged. "Isn't it?"

"No!" All this time he was fighting an attraction to her and she thought he didn't like her? "I'm just trying to keep a sense of dignity for my office. Decorum."

"I don't think it works."

This time he did laugh. "Not with you."

When she didn't reply, the corridor grew quiet. But this quiet was different from what he'd felt as he left Constanzo in the den. This quiet hummed with electricity.

He liked her. He didn't want to like her but he did. And he wanted to kiss her.

He took another step closer. She looked up at him, her blue eyes wide and unsure. Temptation whispered through him. Once, just once, be with somebody who might truly understand. Be honest. Be yourself.

Her eyebrows rose.

Was she asking him to kiss her?

His gaze dropped to her mouth then returned to her eyes. He could imagine the smoothness of her succulent lips, see every move he'd make in his mind's eye. He wouldn't be gentle. She wasn't gentle. She was open, frank, honest. He would kiss her that way.

A second ticked off the clock. Two. Three. He couldn't quite get himself to bend and touch his lips to hers. Not because he didn't want to. But because he so desperately did. An aching need filled his gut, tightened his chest. No one had ever caused feelings like these in him. No one had ever made him want so badly he could see a kiss before it happened.

She whispered, "Good night, Tucker," and turned to grab the doorknob, her fingers trembling.

When she disappeared into her room, a rush of relief swooshed through him. They were wrong for each other. Too different. Nothing would come of them kissing. Especially not a relationship. And without a relationship, a kiss was—unwelcome?

Unwarranted? A smart executive wouldn't open himself to the trouble kissing an employee would bring.

Early the next morning, they climbed into one of Constanzo's cars and headed even farther into the hills. Tucker set the GPS on his phone to Italian and Vivi's mouth dropped.

"You speak Italian?"

He risked a sidelong glance. This morning she wore scruffy jeans that caressed her perfect behind and a pink casual top that brought out the best in her skin tones. After the near-miss with kissing her the night before, his body reacted as if he had a right to be interested, attracted, aroused by her innocent, girl-next-door sexiness.

He told his body to settle down. Yes, she was attractive and, yes, he was interested in her, but only sexually. In every other way they didn't mesh. She had to be off-limits. "You *don't* speak Italian?"

"No."

Yet another thing added to the pile of reasons his attraction to her was ridiculous. "Well, don't worry. Constanzo said his son was raised in the U.S., remember?"

Wind blew in through her open window and tossed strands of her hair across her face. Pulling them away, she asked, "Have you figured out what you're going to say to him?"

"I'm going to flat out tell him who he is."

She gaped at him. "I think that's a mistake!"

And here was the real reason he wouldn't kiss her, knew they'd never have a relationship, knew the taste of her lips that he longed for would only get him into trouble. If he wanted one route, she always wanted another. If that wasn't proof his attraction to her was pointless, he didn't know what was.

"I don't think it's a mistake. If my father had found me, that's how I would want to be told. Up front and honest. I might be angry at first, but eventually I would mellow."

"That just sounds wrong to me."

"Of course it does."

"What if Constanzo's son's not like you? What if he's shy? Or quiet? Artistic types, as Constanzo's file says his son is, aren't like businessmen."

"Oh, and you know a lot about this?"

She shrugged. "I know some. Everybody knows artists aren't like businessmen. Otherwise, they'd be businessmen. They wouldn't be artists."

"Well, if he's a shy starving artist who wears his heart on his sleeve, kick my shin and take over the conversation."

"Me?"

"Hey, Constanzo wanted you here. Maybe this is why." Which was the reason he couldn't put her on his plane and send her back to the accounting department in the Inferno corporate offices in New York. Constanzo might pretend to be an easygoing, open book, but like any clever businessman he had his secrets, his ways of reading people. He'd seen something in Olivia that made him want her here. Tucker wouldn't argue that. He'd use it.

She sighed and eased herself back to her seat. "I agree about kicking your shin, but if I do, you should just shift gears."

"Let me assure you, Miss Prentiss—" he paused and sighed "—*Vivi*, if you kick my shin, you had better have a plan."

The rest of the drive passed in silence until an isolated farmhouse came into view. Not renovated as Constanzo's had been, Antonio's rundown house had seen better days. The manicured grounds of Constanzo's estate were replaced by fields teaming with tall grass and wildflowers.

"Obviously, the guy doesn't own a lawn mower."

"Or he likes nature."

Tucker sniffed a laugh.

"What would you rather paint? A mowed lawn or a field of wildflowers against a blue, blue sky."

Cutting the engine, Tucker rolled his eyes and shoved open his door. Vivi quickly followed suit. Behind Tucker, she picked her way up the loose stone walk. When they reached the door, he knocked three times in rapid succession.

Inhaling a big breath of fresh air, he glanced

around. It really was quiet, peaceful, beautiful. He supposed he could understand why an artist would choose to live here. Especially if he'd come to Italy to get to know his mother's country, to meet his extended family, and still have privacy.

The wooden door swung open. A man about as tall as Constanzo, wearing jeans and no shirt stood before them. "Yeah?"

"I'm Tucker Engle and this is my assistant, Olivia Prentiss."

Vivi reached forward and extended her hand. "It's nice to meet you. You can call me Vivi."

The man cautiously took her hand, his dark eyes narrowing.

"Are you Antonio Signorelli?"

"Yes. Who are you?"

Tucker said, "Can we come in a minute?"

He started closing the door. "Actually, I'm very busy. And I don't have time for sales people."

Wedging his shoe between the door and its frame, Tucker laughed. "We're not sales people. We're here representing—"

Olivia kicked him in the shin. He yelped and jumped back.

She smiled sweetly at Antonio. "We're representing a private collector who's interested in sponsoring a showing of the artwork of someone new and fresh."

Antonio visibly relaxed. "Really?"

"Look how he's dressed?" She angled her

thumb at Tucker and he glanced down at his suit coat and green tie. Sure he was a bit overdressed for the country. But he was a businessman not a hippie.

"I'm okay." She rolled her eyes dramatically. "But he's obviously not a tourist and his clothes are too expensive for him to be a salesman. As I said, we represent a private collector."

"And you want to show *my* work?"

Vivi stepped forward. "Well, we haven't seen your work. Our client is an art patron, but he's not a sap. Your work would have to meet certain standards." She smiled. "We'd love to see it."

As they waited for Antonio to take Vivi's hint and let them in, Tucker scowled. She'd made fun of *his* clothes? Antonio had no shirt. Bare feet. Jeans that hung low on his hips. Sheesh. With his black curly hair tousled, the guy was a walking cologne ad. At least Tucker was fully covered.

Finally, Antonio opened the door wide enough for them to enter. "The place is a mess."

Vivi put her hand on his forearm. "We're not here to see the place. We're here to see your work." She glanced around. "I understand your primary venue is painting."

"Yes."

They entered a house desperately in need of updating. Lines in the plaster and a cracked window were the highlights of the room Antonio led them to. A half-finished painting sat on an easel. But many canvases leaned against the back wall.

The paintings lured Tucker into the room. Vivid colors and stark images dominated. He turned his head slightly and caught Antonio's gaze.

"You have a unique way of looking at the world."

Antonio laughed. "I had a unique upbringing."

Tucker swung his gaze to Olivia. If ever there was an opening to tell him about his father, this was it. But she quickly shook her head.

He sucked back a sigh. She had better know what she was doing.

She turned to Antonio with a smile. "What was unique about your upbringing?"

He shrugged, walked to the stack of paintings where Tucker stood and flipped the first away from the second. "My mom died when I was young." He took painting one and slid it aside so Tucker could more clearly see painting two. "I was raised in foster care."

"So was I." This time he didn't look to Olivia for consent. This was Business Conversation 101. Identify with your client and have them identify with you. "Someone left me in a church." He focused attention on the painting Antonio had bared for him. It was the proverbial field of wildflowers Vivi had talked about. Antonio had painted his backyard and it was stunning. He could almost feel the warmth of the sun, smell the flowers.

Antonio removed painting two, displaying painting three.

Olivia said, "So tell us more about yourself."

"As I said, my mom died." He slid it aside and stood beside Tucker again, patient, as if he'd had others view his work before and knew the drill. "I don't know who my father is. But my mom was from around here. When I got old enough and had saved a few bucks, I came here to meet my relatives." He laughed lightly. "And with landscapes like this to paint, you can see why I never left."

Tucker reverently said, "I can."

Olivia hung back. She didn't have an artist's eye, but she knew the paintings were good. Tucker, on the other hand, clearly thought they were magnificent. But it didn't matter. Her brain had stalled on his quiet statement that he'd been left at a church, didn't know his parents. Her heart broke a little bit picturing a tiny baby, wrapped in a blue blanket, alone for God knows how long in an empty church that had probably echoed with his cries.

But she forced herself to think about business. They'd opened a door for discussions about his parentage and one for displaying his work in a showing. She didn't want to push too hard, too fast. It was time to go.

She stepped forward. "Mr. Engle will give you his cell phone number." She smiled at Antonio, then Tucker. "And you can give us yours." Antonio quickly tore a sheet from a drawing pad and scribbled his number before he handed it to Tucker. He tore off another sheet and offered it to Tucker to write his number too.

Instead Vivi's boss pulled a business card from his jacket pocket.

"You'll be hearing from us."

Antonio beamed. "Great."

The second they were in the car, Tucker turned on her. "What the hell was that all about? We could have stayed there for hours, asked a million questions. He loved us. He'd have done anything we wanted."

"We're supposed to be scouting, not hiring him on the spot. I wanted this to look real."

"There were at least three chances for us to have 'the' real conversation. I could have easily told him who he was."

"And he could have easily turned on us. He's proud of his work. You seemed to agree with his assessment that it's very good. We'll go back to Constanzo's, tell him my plan, see if he likes it. If he does, we ease into Antonio's life over the next few days and ease Constanzo into the art show plan. When the moment is right, we'll tell him."

"Do you know how many ways that could go wrong?"

"Yes. But I also know that if we do it my way, give them a little time together before we drop the bomb, even if he freaks and heads for the hills, he'll still know his dad and when he calms down he could come back."

Tucker started the car. "You'd better be right."

"I may not be."

He gaped at her.

"But I think my plan is better than just dropping him in a pot of boiling water." She peeked over at him. "You know the rule about cooking a live frog don't you?"

His eyes narrowed.

"You put him in warm water, water he's comfortable with and turn up the heat so gradually he doesn't even realize the water is boiling until it's too late."

He shook his head, but didn't argue.

Vivi relaxed. "So, how did you learn about art? Anything looks good to me. I mean, it was clear Antonio's work was good, but I couldn't tell you if it was exceptional. Yet you knew it was."

"It's in the eye of the beholder. If the technique is good, you just check your gut…did it touch you, say something?"

"And what did his work say to you?"

Tucker turned onto the country road again, heading back to Constanzo's. Seconds ticked off the clock. Then a minute. Vivi wondered if he was going to reply to her question.

Just as she was about to ask again, he sighed. "His work tells me that he sees beauty even in an ugly world."

"He thinks the world is ugly?"

"He *knows* the world is ugly. He was raised as a foster kid, remember? Even the foster parents who loved him probably gave him up from time to time, depending upon their own conditions. A foster dad can need heart surgery or a knee replacement. Sometimes they just can't keep you. When he turned eighteen, government help ended. And it's possible he might have suddenly found himself out on the street."

He spoke with such confidence, such surety, that her heart melted a bit. She pictured the baby in the blue blanket, crying in the church again. "I'm guessing some of that happened to you."

He sighed. "I'm not special and I'm not crazily depressed. Things like that happen to a lot of kids. Growing up as a foster kid isn't easy."

"But you made something of yourself."

"Yes, I did."

"And you still think the world is ugly?"

"I think the world is hard, not a sweet soft place like you do."

She gasped. "Are you calling me a Pollyanna? I'm not a Pollyanna!"

He sniffed a laugh. "Right."

"There are things in my past, too."

"Uh-huh. The law suit."

Her chin lifted. "It was humiliating."

"And I'm sure it probably scared you. But I also know the kid dropped his suit. And I'm pretty sure your two parents cuddled you the whole way through it."

"Well, you snob!"

His mouth fell open. "Snob?"

"Do you think everybody with parents had it easy?"

"Certainly easier than those of us who didn't have parents."

"Parents can't fix everything."

"And what happened to poor Miss Vivi that couldn't be fixed? Boyfriend break your heart?"

"My boyfriend turned out to be nothing like everybody thought he was."

"So you called him evil names, his parents sued and you ended up the bad girl."

"Leave it alone."

He sucked in a breath, suddenly so curious he couldn't stop himself. All along he'd recognized there was something about her, something different, something important. And he *knew* it had something to do with that lawsuit. Yet she wouldn't tell him. She pushed and pushed and pushed to hear everything about his life. And he'd coughed up one fact after another. Yet here she was refusing to tell him something he could probably find for himself.

"I could look it up."

She blanched. "Don't. This is painful for me, as painful as your past is to you."

He pulled the car to the side of the road and cut

the engine. "Seriously? You have some kind of teenage Romeo and Juliet thing happen to you and think you can compare it to being left in a church? Abandoned? Raised by people who only took care of you because the state gave them money?"

She licked her lips.

"Come on. You started this. You ask me questions all the time. Now I'm pushing you. What the hell did this kid do that was so bad you had to try to ruin his reputation and force his parents to sue you?"

She glanced down at her hands. "He attacked me. He would have raped me if I hadn't been able to get away."

Tucker froze for three seconds before regret poured through him like hot maple syrup. "Oh, my God. He attacked you?"

"And the thing I did that was so bad that his parents sued? I tried to have him prosecuted."

He'd never felt this combination of remorse and fury before, and had no idea how to deal with it. For every bit as much as he wished he could take back his angry words, he also wanted to punch the kid who'd hurt her. "I'm so sorry."

"We were dating. Everybody assumed we were doing it. After all, he was the star quarterback on the local college football team. Handsome. Wealthy. Every girl in town wanted to date him and he picked me."

"You don't have to go on."

She pulled herself together. Right before his eyes she went from being weak and vulnerable, to being Vivi. His sassy assistant. "Oh, why not? After all, you can look it up."

Regret slithered through him. "I didn't mean it. I'm sorry that I pushed."

"You wanted to know. Now you know."

And he suddenly got it. Her impertinence, her sassiness was a defense mechanism. She'd rather be bossy, pushy, than weak.

Right now, to make up for his stupidity, all he had to do was give her that. Deal with her bossiness, her sassiness rather than her pain.

"Whatever." It physically hurt to downplay her experience, but he knew that's what she wanted. She'd rather be sassy than weak. "You'd just better be sure you're right about Antonio."

"I'm right."

"And you're the one explaining this to Constanzo."

She straightened her shoulders. "I have no problem with that."

"Fine."

"Fine."

The determination in her voice should have heartened him, but he kept picturing her at nineteen, innocent, trusting…and some kid, some smart-assed small-town bully with parents who thought he could do no wrong…accosting her.

It was everything he could do not to beat his hand against his steering wheel.

Especially since he was the one who'd brought up those memories for her.

CHAPTER SEVEN

CONSTANZO MET THEM at the door of his lavish home. "So?"

"So, we met your son."

After their conversation in the car, Vivi was abundantly glad Tucker was a workaholic who thought of nothing but his business. Any day of the week, she'd rather think about work than her past. He didn't care that he'd ripped open old wounds. He didn't care that her nerves were shattered, her brain was numb. He'd pushed for answers and he'd gotten them. Then he'd moved on, leaving her to deal with the repercussions.

Yet another reason to ignore the attraction that hummed between them.

Constanzo motioned for them to follow him back down the hall. "You met my son and—?"

"And he's a gifted artist. Your friend *Vivi* made up a story about you wanting to do a showing for a promising artist and he was one of the people we were checking out. He ate it up like candy on a spoon."

As they reached a living room with soft white sofas, modern-print area rugs, a stunning stone fireplace and a wall of windows that displayed the pool, Constanzo faced her. "Is this so?"

She winced. As if it wasn't bad enough she'd just told the guy she had feelings for about the most horrific thing ever to happen to her, and he hadn't shown her one ounce of compassion, now he'd fed her to the lions.

"I just felt he would need time to get to know you before we dropped the bomb that you're his dad. We can bring him here every day to look at your house and figure out how he'd like to show his paintings here—"

Constanzo shook his head. "No. No. If we do this, we do it right. We rent a gallery with a curator who will do a real showing." He glanced at Tucker. "His work is good enough for this?"

"His work is amazing."

When a gleam of happiness came to Constanzo's eyes, Vivi's heart stopped. She forgot all about her discussion with Tucker in the car. She forgot her worries that she'd handled everything badly. She just saw that gleam.

"You, Vivi, are every bit as bright as I believed you were."

Tucker snorted a laugh as Constanzo walked to the bar. "You disagree with her plan?"

He shrugged. "I'm cautiously optimistic because I want this to work. But I would have just told him."

Constanzo reached for a bottle of Scotch. "I like Vivi's way better." He pulled out three glasses and poured. "So when do I meet him?"

Filled with euphoria that felt a lot like walking on air, she happily said, "Whenever you want."

Handing a glass to Vivi and then Tucker, he said, "I think I would like tomorrow."

Tucker said, "Whoa, Constanzo. We have a lot of work to do first."

"Such as?"

"Getting the gallery for one," Vivi reminded him.

"I have friends and money. I'll have a place for you tomorrow."

Vivi smiled. "Then as soon as the curator is ready for a trip to Antonio's that's when we'll go. But, remember, you can't tell him you're his dad."

"Not even if things are going well?"

"He needs to get to know you." She pulled her lower lip between her teeth. "And, honestly, Mr. B., I think you need to get to know him, too. You're a wealthy man and he's very poor. What if he's a hustler?"

Constanzo's lips turned down. "You think my own son would cheat me." He waved his hands. "Of course, he might. We don't really know who he is."

"Exactly. That's why I figured it was best to

keep who you are a secret until you know each other better."

Constanzo pulled out his cell phone. "We will start tomorrow."

Twenty minutes later Constanzo had a gallery booked and the owner coming to his house the following morning. They toasted with Scotch, which Vivi hated, had lunch, then played pool until it was time to dress for dinner.

Vivi had never seen anyone as happy or animated as Constanzo was that day. But after an afternoon of sipping Scotch, he drank a little too much wine at dinner and left the table early.

Alone with Tucker in the silent dining room, their discussion in the car came tumbling back to her. But a funny thing happened. Before those thoughts could take root—thoughts of Cord and the shame and humiliation of being attacked then sued and bullied when she'd done nothing wrong—she remembered the happiness in Constanzo's eyes. And she felt strong again. Yes, she was disappointed in Tucker pushing her then behaving as if her pain was inconsequential, but that just pointed out what she'd always realized. They weren't good for each other.

As if confirming that, she and Tucker ate their dessert in near silence. She was abundantly glad when her last bite of cobbler was finished and she could excuse herself. She headed toward the stairs and her bedroom, but she wasn't tired.

She didn't really know what she was. Part of her was excited about Antonio and her plan. The other part was really disappointed in Tucker. But her mind no longer automatically jumped to Cord. What he would think. How he would feel about her success. It was like all of that no longer mattered. And that confused her even more.

Maybe she just needed some fresh air?

She turned from the stairs and walked toward the big formal living room with access to the pool. A few lights broke up the darkness and created sporadic twinkles on the blue water, but the area itself wasn't lit. Using her memory of the patio, she found her way to the nearest chaise, sat and stretched out.

"Nice night to just sit outside and look at the stars."

She almost jumped out of her skin. "Tucker! For the love of God! You couldn't have given me a warning you were already out here?"

"That was the purpose of my comment."

She could barely make out his long legs on the chaise, though his shiny black shoes picked up a bit of the light from the well-spaced fixtures around the patio. His white shirt was a lot easier to see. When her gaze reached his face, he smiled.

"You did a good job today."

She sniffed in disdain. "I thought you didn't like my idea."

"I don't. I'd rather bulldoze this thing and get

it done. But Constanzo likes your plan and he's the client, the one we have to please." He toasted her with a drink he must have brought from their dinner table. "And you pleased him."

Syrupy warmth filled her and she relaxed a bit on the chaise. It was really difficult to stay disappointed in a guy who seemed genuinely pleased with her work that day. And maybe how she felt about him didn't matter? It wasn't like they were friends. They were boss and employee.

Plus, bright white stars twinkled overhead. A breeze chilled the night air. She didn't want to go inside yet.

"My only concern is that he's too happy. You do know how easily this plan could backfire."

She frowned. "I can think of about three ways. First, Antonio could dislike Constanzo."

"Constanzo could dislike Antonio."

"Or Constanzo could adore his son—"

"Who might be furious when he learns Constanzo is the father who abandoned him."

She studied the stars. "But he didn't really abandon him. If you listen to the story, Antonio's mother gave up after one measly attempt to contact him."

Tucker chuckled. "Miss Prentiss, I don't think I need to remind you of a little thing called pride."

Her face scrunched in confusion as she considered that. Finally, she said, "So you're saying

Antonio's mother got her feelings hurt so she kept Constanzo's son from him?"

"Exactly."

"Sounds petty."

"Really?" He rolled onto his side. "What if you, poor as you are right now, got pregnant by a man with billions of dollars? A man so far out of your stratosphere that even if he believed your baby was his, he'd question your motives. He'd make you feel cheap and like a gold digger who'd deliberately gotten pregnant for money."

Her face heated. He could be describing the two of them. He was rich. She was poor. And the implications of what he said brought her to her senses very quickly. Forget about his pushing her in the car that day. *This* was why she'd stay away from him, why she should have stayed away from Cord. He hadn't needed to be insensitive with her that morning. Women with no money, no social status, always got burned when they got involved with wealthy men. She'd learned that lesson the hard way and she wouldn't forget it.

"I don't have to worry about that."

"Really?"

"Come on, *Tucker,*" she said, deliberately using his first name because, as with the conversation in the car, he was pushing her buttons again. "I know my place. Billionaires can have their pick of women. They don't go for the dirt-poor, average-looking waifs. They go after the beauties."

He laughed. "Really? You're gonna toss that at me?"

"Toss what?"

"An underestimation of your self-worth."

She blew out a laugh. "I know who I am and what I look like."

"You seriously don't think you're beautiful?"

"Beautiful?" She laughed. "I'll give you pretty. But only when I wear makeup. Which I don't."

"You don't need it."

She laughed gaily at the stupidity of this conversation. Though they were talking about her, it was much better than worry over Constanzo and Antonio or speculating about Antonio's mom. "According to Maria Bartulocci I do."

"Maria was very clearly angling that day. She wanted my attention and she wanted a commission for getting me close to Constanzo. If she put you down, it was to make sure she didn't have competition."

"Competition?" She snorted. "Maria knows she's a beautiful woman."

"You think?"

"You don't?"

He shook his head.

Her eyes widened. "You seriously don't think she's beautiful?"

He snorted. "How would I know? Underneath all that makeup she could have the face of a howler monkey."

"Howler monkey?" Vivi gaped at him. "That was mean!"

"No. That was honest."

She heard the sound of him shuffling on his seat and turned to see he'd sat up and was facing her.

"What I did to you this morning…pushing you to talk when you didn't want to…that was mean."

She was glad for the darkness so he couldn't see the pleasure that came to her face at his apology. Just as at the Jason Jones signing, his behavior proved he wasn't such a bad guy after all. "You didn't know."

"No. I didn't, but I should have suspected something serious had happened from the law suit. You wouldn't have just called somebody a name on the street or harassed someone. You're not a flippant girl, Olivia."

Her heart stuttered, filled with warmth. Not only did he believe her, but no one ever called her Olivia. No one. The way her name came off his lips was sensual, mesmerizing.

"You try to be flippant. You use your sassing as a way to make people think you're in control. Then you turn around and ask a million questions, proving you're not."

Good Lord. No wonder he was rich. He saw right through a strategy that had worked for years. She wasn't sure if she was pleased or frightened.

"There's nothing wrong with asking questions.

It's a good idea to try to get a handle on what's going on when you're confused. But you really should ditch the sassing."

She laughed, but kept her gaze averted.

He caught her chin and forced her to look at him. "I am sorry about this morning."

The smoothness of his fingers against her skin nearly made her shiver. And his eyes—those striking green eyes that saw everything—held her prisoner. Her heart trembled with longing. She hadn't even kissed a guy in years and she desperately wanted him to kiss her. A short, sweet, simple kiss…or a kiss filled with passion and honesty. She didn't care. She just wanted a kiss.

But that was wrong. As she'd begun recovering from Cord, she'd promised herself that she'd never again put herself in the position of being with a man so far beyond her socially. And she'd meant it.

So it was best to let him off the hook about pushing her and return them to their normal relationship. "It's okay."

He sighed and rose from his chaise. "No. It's not."

"Yeah. It is." She rose, too. "You see, when we got back to Constanzo's and we started talking about his son, all those emotions you had dredged up were eclipsed by the feeling of pride I had over doing a good job with Antonio."

He stopped a few feet short of the pool and faced her. "So you're okay?"

She shrugged. "I've been okay for a while. But it felt different—better—that I could totally forget it once we started talking about work."

"So demanding answers from you was a good thing?"

She laughed. "Don't push your luck."

Somehow they'd ended up standing face-to-face again. Under the luxurious blanket of stars, next to the twinkling blue water, the only sound the slight hum of the filter for the pool.

He reached out and cupped the side of her face. "You are a brave, funny woman, Miss Prentiss."

Though she knew it was dangerous to get too personal with him, especially since his nearness already had her heart thrumming and her knees weak, she was only human. And even if it was a teeny tiny inconsequential thing, she didn't want to give up the one innocent pleasure she was allowed to get from him.

She caught his gaze. "Olivia."

"Excuse me?"

"I like it when you call me Olivia."

He took a step closer. "Really?"

She shrugged, trying to make light of her request. "Everybody calls me Vivi. Sometimes it makes me feel six again. Being called Olivia makes me feel like an adult."

"Or a woman."

The way he said *woman* sent heat rushing through her. Once again, he'd seen right through her ploy and might even realize she was attracted to him—

Oh, who was she kidding? He *knew* she was attracted to him. After the episode playing pool the night before, neither one of them could be coy anymore.

Even as yearning nudged her to be bold, reality intruded. The guy she finally, finally wanted to trust was rich, sophisticated and so far out of her league she was lucky to be working for him. She knew better than to get romantically involved with someone like him.

She stepped back. "I wouldn't go that far."

He caught her hand and tugged her to him. "I would." He kissed her so quickly that her knees nearly buckled and her brain reeled. She could have panicked. Could have told him to go slow because she hadn't done this in a while, or even stop because this was wrong. But nobody, no kiss, had ever made her feel the warm, wonderful, scary sensations saturating her entire being right now. Not just her body, but her soul.

His lips moved over hers smoothly, expertly, shooting fire and ice down her spine. Her breath froze in her chest. Then he opened his mouth over hers and her lips automatically parted.

The fire and ice shooting down her spine exploded in her middle, reminding her of where this would go if she didn't stop him. Now. Just as Antonio's mom had been, she was poor. Very far out of Tucker's league. It was foolish to even consider kissing him.

She jerked away, stepped back. His glistening green eyes had narrowed with confusion. He didn't understand why she'd stopped him.

Longing warred with truth. If he could pretend their stations in life didn't matter, she could pretend, too. Couldn't she?

No!

She'd done this before. She was a small-town girl and he was a man of wealth and power. She might be nothing more to him than a conquest. She was too wounded, too cautious to take the risk that someone like him could be serious about someone like her.

She took another step back. "Well, okay then. I guess I'll see you at breakfast."

It was the stupidest, most inane thing she could have said but she took pride in having any voice at all as she turned and raced to her room. She closed the door and leaned against it. She hadn't even kissed a man in years, but in another thirty seconds, she would have willingly let him take her. A man she barely knew. A man with whom she had nothing in common. A man who might only want sex from her. Hell, she wasn't even sure he liked her. Yes, he was attracted to her, but it never really seemed that he liked her.

And her feelings for him? Well, they were getting out of control and she had no idea how to stop them.

CHAPTER EIGHT

THE NEXT MORNING, THE FULL idiocy of what she had said—and done, she couldn't forget she'd run from the patio—hit her, and when she went downstairs for breakfast she had to steady herself outside the dining room door.

She ran her damp palms down the skirt of her second sundress, grateful to have her favorite dress to wear for confidence. But that didn't help much now that she was two seconds away from seeing the man she'd kissed last night, the man she was growing to like, even though it was wrong.

She didn't know how to stop any of this. Her fears after being attacked had robbed her of the normal dating experiences most women had. Though those fears were subsiding and Tucker was making her long for things most women took for granted, she knew—absolutely knew—she was going to get hurt.

Still, she had to go in. If she didn't, it would only make things worse. With a deep breath, she held her head high and stepped into the dining room to find Constanzo and Tucker reading the paper.

Constanzo rose. "Sweet Vivi, good morning."

He pulled out her chair and helped her sit. When he returned to his seat, Tucker looked up from the newspaper.

"Good morning...*Olivia*."

Her blood rushed hot through her veins again, but she refused to be embarrassed or even think through what it might mean. Had he taken her request to heart that she liked to be called by her first name? Or was he taunting her? Reminding her of a kiss that had warmed her blood and made her feel like a woman just as he'd suggested the night before.

Constanzo's maid brought a woman who looked to be about thirty into the dining room. Wearing a suit that had to be handmade and carrying a Gucci bag, she could have given Maria Bartulocci a run for her money.

Constanzo jumped up again. "Patrice!" He caught her hands and kissed both of her cheeks. "Tucker, Vivi, this is Patrice Russo."

After shaking both their hands, she said something to Constanzo in Italian. Constanzo smiled. "Tucker speaks Italian. Vivi, no."

"Then we speak English."

Constanzo pulled out a chair for Patrice. "Would you like breakfast?"

Send For
2 FREE BOOKS
Today!

I accept your offer!

Please send me two
free novels and two mystery
gifts (gifts worth about $10).
I understand that these books
are completely free—even
the shipping and handling will
be paid—and I am under no
obligation to purchase anything,
ever, as explained on the back
of this card.

119/319 HDL F4Z9

Please Print

FIRST NAME

LAST NAME

ADDRESS

APT.#   CITY

STATE/PROV.   ZIP/POSTAL CODE

Visit us online at
www.ReaderService.com

Offer limited to one per household and not applicable to series that subscriber is currently receiving.
Your Privacy—The Harlequin Reader Service is committed to protecting your privacy. Our Privacy Policy is available
online at www.ReaderService.com or upon request from the Harlequin Reader Service. We make a portion of our
mailing list available to reputable third parties that offer products we believe may interest you. If you prefer that we
not exchange your name with third parties, or if you wish to clarify or modify your communication preferences, please
visit us at www.ReaderService.com/consumerschoice or write to us at Harlequin Reader Service Preference Service,
P.O. Box 9062, Buffalo, NY 14240-9062. Include your complete name and address.

HRLP-1/14-GF-13

Send For
2 FREE BOOKS
Today!

I accept your offer!

Please send me two
free novels and two mystery
gifts (gifts worth about $10).
I understand that these books
are completely free—even
the shipping and handling will
be paid—and I am under no
obligation to purchase anything,
ever, as explained on the back
of this card.

119/319 HDL F4Z9

Please Print

FIRST NAME

LAST NAME

ADDRESS

APT.#   CITY

STATE/PROV.   ZIP/POSTAL CODE

Visit us online at
www.ReaderService.com

Offer limited to one per household and not applicable to series that subscriber is currently receiving.
Your Privacy—The Harlequin Reader Service is committed to protecting your privacy. Our Privacy Policy is available
online at www.ReaderService.com or upon request from the Harlequin Reader Service. We make a portion of our
mailing list available to reputable third parties that offer products we believe may interest you. If you prefer that we
not exchange your name with third parties, or if you wish to clarify or modify your communication preferences, please
visit us at www.ReaderService.com/consumerschoice or write to us at Harlequin Reader Service Preference Service,
P.O. Box 9062, Buffalo, NY 14240-9062. Include your complete name and address.

HRLP-1/14-GF-13

"Just coffee." She smiled at Vivi. "So you are my contact."

"Actually, Mr. Engle is in charge of the project." She glanced at him briefly, long enough to see his eyes narrow as she spoke. Embarrassment flared. Why couldn't she have thought of something suave, something sophisticated to say before she'd ran from him and his earth-shattering kiss? Why couldn't she have sashayed into the house as if the kiss had meant nothing?

Taking his seat, Constanzo laughed. "She is modest, our Vivi. This is her plan."

Vivi's gaze shot to Tucker again. He turned his attention to his breakfast. "It is her plan. And Antonio seems to respond to her. She *should* be your contact."

A serving girl poured coffee for Patrice, and Vivi explained her idea. Patrice very quickly outlined the process of bringing an artist's work to a gallery for a showing.

"The very least amount of time we'd need would be two weeks. But I'd suggest a month. We'll spend the first week ironing out the details of our agreement and then I'll take three weeks to choose paintings and get things set up."

"Sounds great."

After finishing breakfast, they wasted no time. Constanzo called for a limo to be brought out front. Vivi and Patrice entered first. Constanzo slid in and sat beside Patrice. Tucker automatically sat beside Vivi. No hesitation. No comment. No complaint.

Knowing it would look childish to slide as far away from him as she could, she stayed where she was, but it was torture. The vague scent of him brought back memories of that kiss. Worse, she had no idea what he was thinking. Had he even liked kissing her? Did he think she was an idiot?

Probably.

When Antonio answered the door, Patrice took over, stepping forward and shaking his hand. "Antonio! It's wonderful to meet you. Mr. Engle and his assistant, Miss Prentiss, raved about your work and we knew we had our artist for the showing Mr. Bartulocci wants to do." She stopped talking, turned to Constanzo and brought him forward. "This is Constanzo Bartulocci. He is your benefactor for the show we'd like to put together."

Tears filled Constanzo's eyes and Vivi blinked back a few of her own. He was meeting his child, his *son,* the person who should be heir to everything he owned. The person who should be filling his quiet life with noise and love and laughter.

Antonio held out his hand. "It's a pleasure to meet you."

Composing himself, Constanzo shook his hand. "It's good to meet you, too." He pulled in a quick breath and smiled. "So where are these remarkable paintings?"

Antonio laughed. "I don't know about remarkable."

Tucker said, "Antonio, this is no time for modesty. Hundreds of people will come to your showing expecting a man confident about what he's done. Confident that he's made a statement. You need to be that guy."

Antonio laughed again and Vivi, Tucker, Constanzo and Patrice followed him into the room he referred to as his painting room.

Patrice looked at the pictures then glanced at Tucker. "You're right. They're splendid."

Relief wove through her voice, but Vivi's nerve endings crackled anyway. Maria Bartulocci definitely wasn't Tucker's type but pretty, stylish, educated blonde and beautiful Patrice? Tucker belonged with somebody like her.

She drew in a quiet breath and told herself not to care as she walked over to Antonio. Tucker and Patrice lost themselves in discussions about his paintings and Antonio looked a bit like he was going to throw up.

"First time having anybody see your work?"

"No. I had a lot of interest in New York, but nothing ever panned out."

Constanzo put his hand on Antonio's shoulder. "This will pan out. We'll do the showing. People will love your paintings. This time next month, you could be famous."

"I don't want to be famous. I want to paint... and eat." He laughed nervously.

Constanzo frowned. "Don't you want people to enjoy what you've done?"

"Yes."

Like a father, Constanzo softly said, "Then this is all good."

Vivi said, "You'll be fine. You'll simply have to figure out how to strike a balance between fame and a private life. Lots of people do it."

"Thanks."

They spent another hour looking at the paintings and talking with Antonio. Before they left, Patrice gave him her card and told him to be at her office the following day to sign papers. Constanzo explained that because he was footing the bill for the showing, Antonio would get every cent paid for any of his paintings, minus the commission for Patrice's gallery. But there was still a need for a formal agreement.

As a precaution, Tucker had Patrice email the agreements for him to peruse that night. They arrived in his in-box right at dinnertime, but Tucker told Constanzo he wasn't hungry anyway. He stayed in his room all night, and Vivi was sure he thought her so much of a ninny he didn't even want to be in the same room if possible.

But he came to breakfast the next morning and seated himself. "You've given your son quite a good deal."

Constanzo laughed. "Of course, I have."

Vivi relaxed. "So, we're paving the way for you to tell your son who you are."

"I don't think we're quite ready for that yet."

Her gaze shot up and over to Tucker. But Constanzo laughed. "You've switched sides." He pointed at Vivi. "First you wanted to hold back and he wanted to tell." He faced Tucker. "Now you want to hold back and she wants to tell."

"Whatever Olivia wants is fine."

She quickly looked away. "Since we started off slowly maybe we should continue to move slowly." But when she risked a peek at Tucker a few minutes later, he was still watching her, studying her.

After breakfast they took the limo to retrieve Antonio then drove along twisting country roads to Bordighera. Cobblestone streets and walkways took them to Patrice's villa gallery. As they drove, Constanzo pointed out the villa of a British royal, the sites Monet had painted and the homes of two novelists.

When they stepped out of the limo, the June sun washed them in warmth. The sound of the surf caused Vivi to turn and see the ocean.

"It's beautiful."

Antonio said, "Now you can see why I decided to stay."

She laughed and nodded, as Patrice opened the front door of her villa and welcomed them inside.

Vivi glanced around in awe. Rich red Oriental rugs accented the white marble beneath them. White drapes billowed to the floor. Chandeliers were everywhere. Eight or ten paintings hung on each wall. Antique tables held small sculptures and blown glass.

"I can't imagine living here."

"I don't," Patrice said, leading them to a stairway and her office. "Well, technically, I do since I have an apartment on the third floor. But I always thought this villa too beautiful to keep to myself." She smiled at Vivi. "I made it a gallery so I can share it."

They signed the agreements in Patrice's office—a warm, welcoming space, different than the formal rooms of the gallery. Right from the beginning, working for Tucker Engle had been eye-opening, and coming to Italy would probably top her list of favorite things she had done in her lifetime. But standing in a gallery, surrounded by paintings and sculptures, blown glass and jewelry so perfect it had to be displayed as art, was surreal.

Oddly, she felt she belonged here. As if she had come home.

Antonio, Constanzo and Patrice shook hands. Patrice made arrangements to go to Antonio's house the next day to begin selecting paintings. Constanzo suggested dinner at his home to celebrate and though Patrice declined, Antonio happily accepted.

They played pool. Ate dinner outside. Drank Scotch.

And the whole time Tucker watched her.

It made an otherwise enjoyable evening nerve-racking. As early as politely possible, she excused herself and headed for her room. She showered and almost slid into her pajamas but it was still too early to sleep. Knowing the men would spend hours playing games in the den, she put on jeans and a T-shirt and headed for the pool.

This time she saw Tucker standing by the sparkling water before she turned the doorknob to go outside. Boldness surged through her. He'd badgered her until she'd told him about Cord. He'd held her feet to the fire, forcing her to take charge of the Antonio project since they were using her idea. And he'd kissed her.

Then today he'd stared at her all day as if she were some sort of bug under a microscope.

Half of her wanted to go out and brag. Her idea might not have seemed like a good one to him, but he had trusted her with it and it was working. *Her* idea was working. She was not going to fail.

The other half wanted to go out and…well, brag too. But in a sharing way. She wanted to say, "Look what we're doing! Look what we're accomplishing! We're bringing together a lonely dad and his son. Even though we don't seem like we belong together, we are a good team."

But that was actually the point. If she went out there and they celebrated their success, weren't they tempting fate?

He might like her but he didn't want to. Hell, he wasn't even really sure he wanted her as an assistant. Forget about anything else. And she knew the dangers of getting too close to someone so far out of her league.

She took one last longing look at him, standing by the pool, looking as if he might be waiting for her—

She turned and went back to her room.

CHAPTER NINE

THE NEXT DAY they returned to Antonio's with Patrice. As he had the day before, Tucker watched Vivi happily help Antonio as he worked with Patrice, an odd feeling in his gut. When he looked at her and Antonio, he saw a couple. When he thought of himself and Olivia together, he saw a disaster.

So why—two days later—did the memory of her breathy request to call her Olivia still fill him with a yearning so primal, so hot, that he wanted to do more than kiss her?

He had no idea. But sharp need pressed in on him. Something about her appealed to him on an elemental level he'd never experienced before. And maybe it was time he stopped denying it?

Patrice began examining paintings, setting two side by side, and a minute later sending one to a group on the right and the other to a group on the left. A process that Tucker would have thought would take days seemed to be taking minutes.

Finally, she sighed. "Here's the deal. I like them

all. I can put almost half of these in the downstairs of my gallery, but if I open the second floor I could double that number."

Though Tucker thought that was wonderful news, anxiety flitted through Antonio's eyes.

Constanzo apparently didn't notice. His face beamed with pride. "And we will invite everybody. I have ordered my personal assistant to begin a list. I'll have a thousand people at that showing."

This time Antonio looked like he would faint. Olivia caught his arm. "Hey, this is your showing. If you don't want a thousand people, just tell us what you do want."

Tucker frowned. Interesting that she wasn't nervous around Antonio. Only around him. No. Strike that. She wasn't nervous around him either. Except when they were close. Or getting personal. Then she got antsy.

He knew the feeling. Once he'd gotten through puberty no woman had made him nervous or confused. Yet with her everything was weird. Different. Confusing.

Antonio took a breath. "I'd like the doors to be opened and people to come in off the street." He glanced at Vivi. "Because they want to come in. Not because they're invited."

Patrice smiled patiently. "But you also need to advertise. Send out invitations at least for the opening night."

Olivia said, "How about this? We'll send out invitations for the opening. That will let Mr. Bartulocci's friends know he's sponsoring a showing. We'll get RSVPs for the actual opening night and invite the rest to stop by while your pieces are on display."

Pride stirred within Tucker. Once again she saw what everybody else seemed to miss. While Patrice thought about making money and Constanzo had found a way to introduce his son to the world, Olivia watched the star and knew he was falling.

Antonio sucked in a breath. "That sounds a little more doable."

"The goal of your show is to sell your paintings," Patrice reminded him.

"And our goal," Constanzo quietly countered, finally seeing what Vivi had noticed all along, "wasn't to make money but to introduce a wonderful new talent. That's why I'm paying for everything. There's no chance of a loss for you."

Patrice smiled woodenly. "Of course."

Antonio hugged Vivi. "Thanks."

Her face reddened, but her eyes danced with pleasure. Still, she didn't get the look—the look she'd gotten when she'd asked him to call her Olivia. The look that still filled his blood with lust every time he thought of it.

She might like Antonio but she wasn't interested in him. Not the way she was interested in Tucker.

Constanzo chatted through the entire limo ride. But when they got to his house, his maid approached him with a message. He read it then excused himself to make a call. Olivia went to her room. Tucker ambled back to the den, poured himself a draft and threw a few darts before Constanzo joined him.

"I'm afraid I have some bad news."

Tucker turned from the dart board. "Bad news?"

"The call I had to return was to Maria." He winced. "She's managed to get herself into a bit of trouble with her mother. It's nothing that a visit from me won't cure but it's also not something I'd expect my guests to endure."

Tucker laughed.

"So you and Vivi have the whole house to yourselves tonight. I've instructed the cook to make spaghetti Bolognese for dinner. Serve it with the Sangiovese. Make yourselves at home."

"Thanks." Anticipation pricked his nerve endings. He and Olivia would be alone? They hadn't had two minutes alone since that kiss...

Maybe it was time they did?

Knowing Olivia was already nervous around him, he decided not to tell her. When she went to the pool, he returned to his room to read emails and make calls.

He checked on dinner before showering and changing into trousers and a white shirt, which he left open at the throat. No tie. No sport coat.

Nothing to make her feel—what had she said? Less than?

When she arrived in the dining room he had the Sangiovese breathing. She immediately noticed only two places had been set at the table and she stopped a few feet away from her seat.

Her gaze swung to his. "Just you and me?"

Downplaying the significance of that, since he didn't want her running before they had a chance to talk about that kiss, he walked over and pulled out her chair. "It seems Maria's gotten herself into some trouble with her mother. Constanzo has to smooth ruffled feathers."

She laughed lightly as she sat. "It's kind of funny to think of Maria as being in trouble with her mom. She doesn't seem like the kind of woman who answers to anyone."

"Everybody answers to someone."

She laughed again. "Yeah. With my parents I think I know that better than anyone." She paused until he sat at the place across from her. "You do know they came to check up on you the day they visited New York?"

This time he laughed. "I'm sure I made a stellar impression." But even as he said that, an odd realization came to him. He'd never met a girlfriend's parents. Not one. Because he didn't really have girlfriends. He had dates—lovers.

"Good enough that my parents trusted me to go to Italy with you." She winced. "Of course, I had to do some persuading, but in the end they trusted you."

He sucked in a breath. Strange feelings tumbled around in his gut. No parents in their right minds should trust their beautiful, naive daughter to him—

Unless they expected him to behave like a gentleman? To them, Olivia wasn't a "date" or a "lover". She was their daughter. Their little girl and they would expect him to treat her as such.

The maid brought their salads and garlic bread. After she was gone, Olivia tasted her salad and groaned. "That is fantastic. I'm going to have to diet when we get home."

"Then you probably don't want to know that our main course is spaghetti Bolognese."

She groaned again and set down the garlic bread. "I'll focus on the salad so I have room for the spaghetti."

They ate in silence for a few seconds, then she glanced around. "My mother would probably love Italy."

More talk of her parents, more of those uncomfortable feelings. "Really?"

"My mom likes things with roots. Family recipes. Older houses. She researched our house after she and Dad bought it. Found relatives of the woman who had owned it, and got some of the family recipes." She took a bite of salad, chewed and swallowed. "She said preparing those dishes was like keeping that family alive, too. She respects the sense of continuity."

He smiled, but discomfort graduated to awkwardness. He didn't even know who his parents were. He'd tried to find them a few years back, but there were no clues. He was a baby left alone in a church. Generic blanket. Department-store bottle and diapers. There was no way to find them. He had no parents, no pictures. No old family recipes. No sense of continuity.

"That—" He paused. Not having a normal family had always bothered him from the perspective of not having a support system. But from the way Olivia talked about her mother it was clear she was her friend. They were close. Loving. Impossible for him to comprehend. "That sounds nice."

"It is nice." She laughed. "She's quite the mother hen."

He poured more wine. "What about your dad?"

"Oh, he's our big teddy bear. He doesn't say a lot but we always know he loves us, you know?"

He didn't. He'd never *known* anyone loved him. In fact, in spite of the declarations of a few lovers, he didn't think anyone had actually loved him.

"He's also a card player. When we lose electricity in an ice storm, he always starts a candlelight game of Texas Hold'em or rummy."

Which explained why she had been so comfortable playing rummy with Constanzo the day she'd met him.

"Your dad gambled with you?"

"We'd play for candy."

"Sounds nice." Again. He could envision her family huddled around a table, playing a game by candlelight. Laughing. Just enjoying each other's company. The thought twisted his heart but teased his imagination.

"What about holidays?" He really shouldn't ask. Hearing her stories only reminded him of what he didn't have, but he couldn't resist. In the same way she tempted him, so did thoughts of a family. He'd longed for one as a child, considered the possibility of having one when he tried to track down his parents, then closed the door when he couldn't find them.

Now here he was longing again, just like a little boy with his nose pressed up against a candy-store window.

"My mom's favorite is Easter. She loves pastel colors. Hiding Easter eggs. Going to the Easter-egg hunt sponsored by the volunteer firemen. And though most Americans don't wear hats anymore, she still gets a new one every year for church on Easter Sunday."

He laughed and took a sip of wine.

"But even though she likes Easter the best, my dad's the Christmas freak. Have you ever seen those movies where people try to outdo each other with outdoor lights?"

"I've seen a few."

The spaghetti came. The aroma filled the room and she inhaled deeply. "Wow. That smells fantastic."

"Constanzo promised you some really good food in return for sharing that leftover Chinese food. So far he's made good on his promise."

She winced. "He probably thought I was such a dork. I didn't even have a plate for him. He had to eat out of the box."

"I think he was too hungry to care. Besides, a lot of people like eating food out of boxes. It reminds them of their childhood."

"Does eating food out of boxes remind you of your childhood?"

His chest tightened. He should have realized that she'd turn this discussion to him. She was too polite to monopolize a conversation.

"I don't remember a lot of my childhood."

"I'm sorry. I probably shouldn't have brought that up."

"It's fine." It wasn't. He'd convinced himself to believe his lonely childhood had strengthened him, made him into the strong man he was today, but strength wasn't the only quality a person wanted to have. Knowing her had resurrected his longing for a connection, a place, a real place where he wasn't just wanted and respected, but where he could be himself.

"I'm sure growing up in foster care had to have been difficult."

"It was."

"I shouldn't have brought up Christmas."

"It's fine. Really." He cleared his throat. To salvage his pride, he couldn't let her feel sorry for him. "Some foster families really tried. But they don't get a lot of money from the government to care for the kids they take in so they can't do everything. As a foster child, you adjust."

The room fell silent again. He toyed with his spaghetti. Worried that she still felt bad, he caught her gaze. "But I had some nice Christmases."

Her face brightened. "Did you?"

"Yes. Two. One year when I was about six I really wanted a certain video game. My foster parents already had the game box in the family room that could play the game, so I asked for it knowing I probably wouldn't get it, but they got it for me."

Her eyes warmed. "That's nice."

He thought back to that day. The one day in his childhood when he actually thought life could be wonderful. "It was nice. But because my foster parents had spent so much on the toy, I didn't get the usual clothes I would have gotten as gifts and my jeans wore thin. I spent the rest of the winter wearing shoes with a hole in the bottom."

"Oh."

He cursed himself in his head. Now he knew why he shied away from honesty. It hurt. And not just him. He could actually feel sorrow pouring from her.

And *that* was why he'd always be alone. Or with women who didn't care to know him. No man wanted a woman he lusted after feeling sorry for him.

"You have to be proud of yourself for how far you've come."

"Yes. Of course, I am." He sat straighter on his chair, closed his heart. Forgot about all those longings for the things she'd had and could tell him about. "But it should also make you realize that if you really want to become successful, you shouldn't let anything stand in your way."

He turned the conversation to a discussion of focus and discipline as they finished dinner then excused himself.

The empty, lonely feeling that followed him to his room was an echo of what he'd sensed with Constanzo, and he realized he and the reclusive old billionaire had a lot in common. His refusal to be vulnerable might be the right choice, but at sixty-five or seventy, he was going to wake up one day and find himself every bit as alone as Constanzo was now.

But in some lives there was no choice. Opening up and being honest simply couldn't be done.

Two days later, with Antonio settled and Constanzo thinking he *might* like to be the one to tell

Antonio he was his father, Vivi and Tucker left Italy. After their dinner alone, he'd become quiet. So she wasn't surprised when he handed her work to do on the long flight to New York City.

Hours later they landed at the private airstrip and transferred to his limo. He instructed the driver to take her home first. After a quick, impersonal goodbye, she climbed the three flights of stairs.

When she stepped into her apartment, she was bombarded by hugs and questions from Laura Beth and Eloise. She managed to sidestep the more personal aspects of her trip by focusing on Antonio, her work with a gallery owner and an artist, and her pool games with a billionaire who really would have taken her money if she'd been foolish enough to bet with him.

She told them about the beautiful Italian countryside and then spilled over into a gushing report on Bordighera, which, she told them, they would have to visit—if they ever got enough money to go on a vacation.

She slept like a log, woke groggy, but capable of working, and headed to the office dressed in the gray trousers and pink shirt. No blazer this time. June had turned into July and it was getting hot.

When she arrived at the office, Tucker was already there, head bent over papers on his desk.

She stood by her chair, confused. In a little over

a week she and Tucker Engle had gone from being something like adversaries to—

She didn't know what. Almost friends? He'd apologized for pushing her into talking about something that was none of his business. Hell, she'd told him about something that was none of his business. They'd sat by a swimming pool and talked like normal people.

He'd kissed her.

Then they'd had that wonderful private conversation over the spaghetti Bolognese. He'd told her things about his past. Personal, intimate things. Things that showed her that deep down he was a nice guy, a good guy. Not somebody born to money who abused people. Not somebody she had to fear. But somebody she could trust. Somebody special.

And now they were just supposed to go back to the quiet?

She glanced into his office again. His head was still down. His focus clearly on his work. Wasn't he even going to say good-morning?

Apparently not.

It was sad, painful. Especially considering that that conversation hadn't just shown her she could trust him. It had also caused her to like him. The real him.

Maybe too much.

She turned, slid her backpack beneath her desk. A file sat beside her desktop computer. She opened it to find the financials she'd been reviewing the night before. She lowered herself to the office chair, turned the pages to her stopping point, found the legal pad on which she'd been jotting notes and did what she was supposed to do: looked for inconsistencies. Hot spots. Potential trouble.

But her heart broke. She'd never met anybody like him. Never had an adventure like the one she'd had in Italy. And now they were back to not talking.

Two hours later the elevator bell sent a spike of noise into her silent space, causing her head to snap up. Ricky Langley and Elias Greene walked out. Though disgust rolled through her when she saw Elias, he smiled apologetically. She smiled politely and turned to grab the phone to alert Tucker that they were in her office.

But Tucker was already standing in his doorway. He greeted them without as much as a glance in her direction and closed the door behind them.

She sat back in her chair with a huge sigh. Not speaking *might* work to get them past the awkwardness of their near miss with friendship and their kiss, but it wouldn't do anything to stop her longing for more. If she closed her eyes, she could see the blue Italian sky. The rolling hills. The green grass. The cobblestone streets. The villa gallery.

Her opinions had been important. Antonio had

listened to her advice. Constanzo had treated her like an equal. And Tucker had kissed her.

She traced her fingers over her lips. Every time she thought about that kiss, they tingled. Her whole body came to life as if remembering every single detail of the way his lips felt pressed to hers, the way his tongue felt taking possession of her.

Now here she sat in an office so quiet she could hear her own breathing.

Tucker's meeting with Elias and Ricky lasted an hour, then he took the pair to lunch. She ate a peanut butter and jelly sandwich and drank a bottle of water.

Knowing she had to withdraw money for the week, she left the office in search of an ATM. She punched in her account number and waited for her balance to appear. When it did, it was twelve thousand dollars over what she expected.

Twelve thousand dollars.

Crap. Somebody somewhere had made a mistake and she'd have to fix it.

Knowing she had sufficient cash to cover a meager withdrawal, she retrieved the money she needed and returned to the office to call the bank.

"This is Olivia Prentiss. My checking account number is—" she rattled off her number "—I seem to have too much money. Twelve thousand dollars too much money. You might want to check that out."

The service representative chuckled. "Thank you for calling us. I'm pulling up your account now." She paused. "Hmm…I see a twelve thousand dollar deposit from a company called Inferno." Another pause. "Do you know them?"

She sucked in a breath. "Actually, I work at Inferno." She grimaced. It would probably be better to tell Human Resources about the mistake and let the company handle it. "Never mind. I'll check it out with my boss."

She disconnected the call and was ready to dial the extension for HR, but a strange thought popped into her head. What if it had been Tucker who'd dropped the twelve thousand dollars into her bank account?

And if so, why?

She went over everything that had happened in Italy and stopped when she remembered that kiss. The rush of excitement. The rightness. The swirl of need. The way he took possession of her.

And the cash in her checking account felt like a glaring, horrible insult—a blackmail payment. *Forget everything that happened in Italy.*

Waiting for him to return, she tried to focus on the financials, but the money in her checking account haunted her.

The second the elevator doors opened, she said, "So, what? Were you afraid I'd tell somebody you kissed me? Or afraid I'd tell somebody the things you'd told me while we were eating spaghetti?"

Tucker's face scrunched in confusion. "What?"

"The twelve grand. Is that payment so I'll keep my mouth shut?"

He rubbed his fingers across his forehead as if totally unable to believe what she'd said then he pointed at his door. "My office. Now."

She rose from her seat, her head high, and followed him. He fell to the chair behind the desk. She primly sat on the chair in front of it.

"That kiss meant nothing."

Her heart kicked against her ribs. Just when she thought she couldn't feel any worse, he proved her wrong.

"Well, thanks."

"You can't have it both ways, Miss Prentiss. Either you're insulted enough by the kiss to think I'd need to pay you off, or you liked kissing me."

Heat rose to her face.

He sighed. "The order to get the money into your account went out before we went to Italy. The day we left, HR called and told me there was too big of a disparity between Betsy's salary and yours. We couldn't give you a raise to take you up to Betsy's salary since you won't earn that much in Accounting, so we chose a bonus. Your direct deposit is equivalent to an extra thousand dollars a week while you're filling in for her."

Her mouth hung open. Everybody had told her Betsy would be out eight weeks, ten tops. Now suddenly it was twelve? Twelve weeks with a guy she liked, a guy she'd confided in, a guy she'd kissed…a guy who now hated having her around?

"I can't take it."

"Why not?"

"Because it's not right."

"Betsy makes about three times what you make in Accounting. Adding another thousand dollars a week hardly evens the score. It was a compromise number set by Human Resources. Besides, you earned your keep last week."

"I did very little."

"You understood Antonio. You knew to jump in when he needed someone to intervene."

"We haven't told him Constanzo's his father."

"Constanzo wants the chance to tell him himself. We have to respect that."

"I still don't feel right."

He leaned back and steepled his fingers. Vivi surreptitiously studied him, suddenly realizing why she didn't want to take his money. She wanted him to like her and he didn't. She didn't know why he behaved so different in Italy, but they'd talked honestly. Openly. He'd apologized. She'd explained things to him that she'd only ever told Eloise and Laura Beth. They'd connected.

That's what made him different from Cord. *That's* why she liked him. It wasn't the money or his good looks or even the romantic trip to Italy.

They had connected.

"I don't want your money." She lifted her chin. "I want to go back to what we had in Italy."

"We didn't have anything in Italy."

"Yes, we did. We talked. We got close. You kissed me."

"That was a mistake." Tucker looked away, but he knew this was his opportunity to fix the slip up of kissing her and talking to her, to get the stars out of her eyes and get their relationship back to a professional one.

He deliberately caught her gaze again, held it. "Kisses lead to becoming lovers and if I take a lover it's for scx and sex only."

"I don't believe you."

"You don't have to believe me."

"You *liked* talking to me."

"Maybe, but in that conversation I also realized you like connections. Continuity. You want somebody to connect with long term. Somebody to share your life with, I'm not that man."

"How do you know if you won't even try?"

"Because it's not what I want. And I'm rich enough that I don't have to do things I don't want to do."

He saw the light of recognition come to her eyes. They widened with surprise, then dulled with acceptance. In essence, he'd just dumped her.

She rose. "I still don't want your money." Head high, she walked out of his office.

The relief he expected didn't come. Instead,

his stomach soured with the truth. No matter how much he wanted her, how tempting her body and how alluring her honesty, he couldn't have her. And it was time they both faced that.

CHAPTER TEN

AFTER DAYS OF INTENSE FOCUS on the financials of a company Tucker ultimately decided not to buy, he switched gears and had Vivi looking at the financials of a company he already owned. The weekend came, and, glad for two days off, she did nothing but read.

On Monday morning, she woke with a headache and by the time she got out of the shower she was so dizzy she could barely stand.

Racing out the door, Laura Beth told her to take the day off. Heading into the shower, Eloise agreed. So she unwound her towel and walked to the dresser for clean pajamas. Almost too tired to lift them out of the drawer, she struggled to get the top over her head and the bottom pulled up to her waist.

Exhausted, she fell face first on her bed. Vaguely, she heard the sound of Eloise leaving for that day's interview but that was her last conscious thought.

At twenty till ten, Tucker Engle sat at his desk staring at the phone. He had no idea why Olivia hadn't come into the office today but he had one of those sneaking suspicions she'd told him about.

She was quitting. After almost complete silence between them for days, their only words to each other questions and answers about that day's work, she'd had enough.

He supposed it was her prerogative to leave Inferno, but no matter how close they'd gotten in Italy, how disappointed she was in his ability to return those feelings, she still had to turn in a notice. Two weeks was customary.

He could have Human Resources call her. But what would he do if she told them she was quitting because he'd kissed her? Or she was quitting because they'd connected in Italy and now he refused to be personal with her?

He didn't think she'd do that, but he also didn't want his private business advertised. So he called Human Resources, got her cell phone number and called her.

He waited four rings before the call went to voice mail.

Which probably meant her phone was busy.

He gave her twenty minutes then hit redial. After four rings, it went to voice mail.

Ten minutes later, he hit redial again and it went to voice mail.

Five minutes later, he hit redial. And finally she answered.

"Hello?"

Her weak voice cracked. She sounded like she was on death's door.

Cold fear flooded him. He cursed the feeling. Not just because he wasn't supposed to like her but because he hated anything he couldn't control.

"Are you all right, Miss Prentiss?"

"What?"

The disorientation in her frail voice sent panic through him. But he forced himself to remain professional. "Okay, I'm guessing you're sick."

Nothing.

"Miss Prentiss?"

Nothing.

"Olivia?"

"I'm fine."

No, she wasn't! He could tell from her weak voice that something serious was wrong. He disconnected the call and summoned his driver. The forty minutes it took to get to her apartment increased his panic and he raced into her building. He sighed at the three flights of stairs he had to climb and in the end took them two at a time. When he reached her apartment door, he knocked and knocked. Just as he was considering finding her building superintendent to get a key, the door opened.

Her hair was a tumble of knots. The puffy lids over her glazed eyes drooped. His gaze fell to her soft pink pajamas. The top had thin straps that all but bared her shoulders to him and revealed a plump pink strip of cleavage. The loose bottoms clung to the swell of her hips.

He swallowed hard. He'd never met anyone as naturally beautiful, as naturally built, as she was. And yet she believed she wasn't good enough.

"Well, at least you're not dying."

She looked at him, but said nothing. Tucker wasn't really sure she saw him.

He shepherded her back into her apartment, which was small, but neat and clean. "Which room is yours?"

She pointed back down the hall. That didn't tell him anything, so he let her lead. She passed the first door and turned into the second. One bed was made. The other looked as if a band of feral cats had had a fight under the covers. She fell to the bed with the tousled bedclothes.

Silence fell over the room, the echoing sound of no people. She was alone, sick. Too sick to even get herself a glass of water. And there was no one in this quiet, quiet apartment to help her. The way there hadn't ever been anyone to help him when he was sick. Not that he'd wanted someone to coddle him, but there was an undeniable loneliness, an emptiness to be faced when even a simple cold demonstrated that you didn't have anyone in your life.

He crouched beside her. "What can I do?"

Her face smashed against the pillow, she said, "Go away."

"I'm serious. Can I make you some soup? Get you orange juice?"

"I don't think we have any of those things."

He took out his cell phone. "Not a problem." He called his driver. "Maurice, we're going to need some chicken soup. Find a good deli. Also get a gallon of orange juice, some pain relievers and some flu medications."

He clicked off the call and looked at Olivia. For all practical intents and purposes she was out. He pulled the covers from under her and gently spread them over her. His fingers brushing her soft, soft shoulders caused an awkward fluttering of his heart. His hands paused, fingers skimming the delicate flesh he longed to be allowed to touch, to taste.

He really liked her. But they were so different. And not just about money or social status. He couldn't talk to her. When she tried to get him to tell her about his past, he'd stupidly told her something that had made her feel sorry for him. After that he couldn't tell her anything else. His past hadn't merely been bad; it had left him in the awkward position of being incredibly social in the right crowd and totally unable to be intimate—even with the right person. And *that* was the real reason he wouldn't pursue her. She deserved better.

He walked into the front part of her apartment with a sigh. He'd panicked. Stupidly. Over a case of the flu.

Of course, he hated the thought of anyone being alone and sick. And, more important, he didn't want her to get dehydrated. He needed her to get well enough to return to work. He convinced himself the panic was nothing more serious than his need to have his assistant on the job again. Also giving him a story of explanation to tell Olivia when she questioned him—and she would. He smiled ruefully. She always did.

He opened cupboard doors, looking for tea and eventually found some in the cabinet above a rather fancy-looking coffee machine. For three girls just starting out, they had an odd mix of really, really expensive things and things that appeared to be someone's castoffs.

He prepared the tea and almost took it back down the hall but realized he'd be waking her when Maurice returned with the pain killers and flu meds, and he hated to wake her twice. So he sat on her sofa and drank it himself. Sipping, he picked up his phone and read his emails, but he didn't have a decent attention span, not enough to answer important questions, so he turned on the television.

He sat back on the comfortable red sofa and sipped the tea. By the time Maurice arrived with the soup and medicines, he'd seen two news programs, which he should have considered a waste of time. Instead, he felt more relaxed than he had in years.

He took the soup and meds from Maurice who winced. "You should give her a raise or a bonus or something so she can get into a building with an elevator."

"I tried. She told me I was buying her off."

Maurice's eyebrows rose.

"Trust me. She's an odd, odd woman. And if you're smart you won't try to figure her out."

Maurice chuckled and left. Tucker opened the soup which had cooled during transport. He took that, a spoon, the flu meds and the pain reliever back down the hall to her room. She lay sprawled across the bed, exactly as he had left her.

He marched to the bed. "Come on, now," he said using his outside voice in the hope of waking her. "We can't let you get dehydrated."

She didn't even stir.

He placed the soup and meds on her bedside table, sat on her bed and put his hand to her shoulder, then drew it back as if it had stung him. The softness of her skin always seemed to do him in. But he'd made his decisions. A man who couldn't talk about his past couldn't give a woman like Olivia the kind of love she needed.

But he glanced at her face, her eyelashes fanning against cheeks red with fever, her usually smiling lips a straight line and he wanted to touch her. To help her. He had to do this.

He slid his hand to her shoulder again. "Hey, sick person. I'm here to help you."

The warmth of her fever heated his fingers and hit him right in the heart. She needed him. It almost physically hurt to think of her alone and so sick she could barely blink. So he might as well admit it and do what he'd stayed here to do.

He slid farther onto the bed, put his hands beneath her shoulders and lifted her into a sort of sitting position, leaning against him.

"What do you want first? Soup? Pain meds? Flu meds?"

"Flu meds."

He opened the package and filled the little cup to the appropriate measuring point. But by the time he turned to give it to her she was asleep again. He put the cup to her lips and nudged until she woke and drank. She also took a few sips of juice, but that was it.

He left the room thinking he should go back to the office now. There was nothing else he could do for her. She was fine—safe in her bed—but alone.

The emptiness of being alone rose up in him. Having no one who cared when he was sick. Having no one who really knew him, really cared about him. He couldn't leave her with nothing but the ringing silence of this apartment to keep her company.

With a sigh, he returned to the red sofa, took off his jacket, loosened his tie and turned on the TV again.

Two hours later she staggered into the living room, a blanket wrapped around her.

He shot off the sofa. "Miss Prentiss! Are you sure it's wise for you to be out of bed?"

She made her way over to him. "At this point I'm not entirely sure I'm going to live." She sat on the sofa. "The only reason I have strength enough to get out of bed is the medicine you gave me. Thank you for that, by the way."

He slowly lowered himself beside her. "You're welcome."

"And for coming over."

"I couldn't stand to think of you alone and sick."

She glanced at him. Her eyes told him that she remembered the things he'd said on the trip to Italy, about being a foster child, a baby left in a church in only a blue blanket. A little boy who had once gotten a Christmas gift and that had come at the expense of clothes he'd needed.

She cleared her throat. "Yeah. I get it."

Discomfort turned his muscles to stone. He *hated* that she felt sorry for him. He could not handle pity. And maybe that's why talking to her had scared him more than thoughts of seducing her? People who knew his past might respect him for how he'd changed his life, but deep down inside most people also pitied his humble beginnings. That's why he'd choked on the words and couldn't tell her any more than he already had. He didn't want to be pitied. Especially not by her.

He rose from the sofa and grabbed his suit jacket. "Let's not make a big deal out of it. Are you well enough for me to go back to the office?"

She nodded. "Yes."

"I had Maurice get you chicken soup from a deli. You should eat that and drink plenty of fluids."

She nodded.

He hesitated. With the threat of discussing his past gone, it again felt wrong to leave. She appeared to be well. At least well enough that he knew she could take care of herself, but it just didn't feel right leaving her.

"Are you sure you don't want me to stay and play cards or something?"

She laughed. "You play cards?"

"I do all kinds of normal things."

"I have always suspected as much."

He shook his head. "Even sick you're a smartass."

"You're the boss. You could have gotten rid of me on day one."

Her slightly glassy blue eyes connected with

his and his heart turned around in his chest, like a little kid doing somersaults in a swimming pool.

He liked her so much.

He didn't just think she was pretty or had potential. He *liked* her. That was why he didn't get rid of her, always felt different around her, more alive.

But he didn't share his past with anyone. Ever. He'd tried with her and only ended up evoking her pity.

He stuffed his cell phone in his pocket. "I'll see you when you're better." He walked to the door, but faced her again. "You should call HR tomorrow morning if you're not coming in. They like to keep track of things like that."

He walked out of her apartment, closed the door behind him and squeezed his eyes shut.

He had been perfectly fine, perfectly happy until she'd come into his life. Now he yearned for things he couldn't have…things he'd long ago adjusted to never having.

He wished with every fiber in his being that Betsy could get better so Olivia could return to Accounting and maybe, just maybe, he could forget all this.

A week after her four-day flu, Vivi sat in Tucker's office, straight as an arrow.

Though he'd very sweetly cared for her the first

day she was sick, when she'd recovered, she'd re-turned to a silent workplace, a venue for nothing but labor. He wouldn't accept her thanks for car-ing for her. He didn't want to discuss it. He didn't look at her. Gave her assignments piecemeal, as Mrs. Martin had said he would, and absolutely didn't give any explanations for anything.

She couldn't even measure the disappointment. But she got the message. He didn't want any mis-understanding. He'd cared for her because she was alone. He knew what it was like to be alone, and didn't want to see anybody suffer that fate, but he did not like her.

So why the hell did she continue to like him more and more?

In the silence of his enormous office, the ring of his phone sounded like a bomb going off.

He glanced up at her. "Very few people have this private number. I have to take this."

She nodded and sat back.

He picked up the phone. "Tucker Engle."

"Oh, Tucker!"

"Constanzo? What's up?"

"It's Antonio. He is, as you say, freaking out."

"Did you tell him you're his dad?"

"No! He's just going nuts about the show."

He glanced at Olivia. "Miss Prentiss is here with me. I'm going to put you on speaker."

He hit the button and Constanzo immediately

said, "Vivi! You should be here. You calm him down."

"You can calm him down, Constanzo."

"I can't." The passion in his voice vibrated through the room.

Vivi laughed. "You can. You're just freaking out, too. Take a breath, calm down."

"No, you take a plane, come to me. Help me."

Tucker sat forward. "Actually, that's a very good idea."

Vivi's gaze shot to him. Though she loved being in Italy and working with Antonio, after the way Tucker had behaved these past few weeks his suggestion that she leave felt like a kick out the door.

"I'll have her on the plane in two hours."

"Thank you, my dear friend Tucker!"

He disconnected the call and Vivi stared at him. "Are you trying to get rid of me?"

He wouldn't look at her. "You handle Antonio very well. It's only good common sense to send you over there."

"Antonio is a grown man. So is Constanzo. They could deal with this."

He finally glanced up. "You think?" When she said nothing, he tossed his pen to his desk. "Once again, you underestimate your abilities." He shook his head. "This deal is extremely important to me. Antonio has to be cool, calm and collected when we tell him Constanzo is his dad. You calm him down."

Because she knew that was true, she said nothing.

"I know you're playing it by ear here, but you really are good with people."

After weeks of no conversation, his praise was like balm to her desperate soul. "Thanks."

"But with everything going haywire, it looks like we can't tell Antonio that Constanzo is his dad until the show is over."

"You want to preserve the show?"

"You don't? It's the one solid thing Constanzo is doing for Antonio. Even if he's angry after we tell him Constanzo is his dad, he'll have the showing to look back on. Something that proves to him his dad believed in him. You can't get a much stronger connection than that."

"You're right."

"So you're in Italy for the next two weeks, until the show opening. I'll have the driver here in ten minutes. He'll take you to your apartment to pack and you can be in the air in two hours as I promised."

With that he went back to work.

Vivi slowly rose from her chair, her heart lodged in her throat. She turned away as tears filled her eyes. She really didn't want to go to Italy without him.

She didn't want to go anywhere without him. Do anything without him.

The horrible truth was…she loved him and he was sending her away.

CHAPTER ELEVEN

EAGER TO GET his office back to normal, without a wonderful woman sitting a few feet away, tempting him to try a relationship he knew couldn't work, Tucker immediately called Mrs. Martin in Human Resources, requesting another accountant. In ten minutes, Ward Bancroft stood in front of him.

With dark hair and dressed in a black suit, black shirt and silver tie, the kid was a mini version of Tucker, without the green eyes. His eyes were a watered down whiskey-brown that reminded him of a weasel.

"So, Mr. Bancroft, are you ready to work?"

"Absolutely. You tell me what you need and I'll have it for you in ten minutes."

He eased forward on his chair. Even though he appreciated a bit of enthusiasm, he preferred dignity. "Some assignments require more attention than ten minutes."

"Oh, absolutely! I'm sorry!" To Tucker's horror he seemed to get even more enthusiastic. "You tell me what you need and I will do it in the best possible way."

"Terrific." He shuffled the papers on his desk until he found the background-information sheet he needed. "This company could potentially be a great project. But the financials look a little too good to be true." He handed the sheet across the desk. "I want you to tear their annual statement apart, see what they're hiding."

He nearly snapped to attention. "Yes, sir!"

He headed out of the office and Tucker said, "Close the door on your way out."

"Absolutely," he singsonged.

As the door closed behind him, Tucker rolled his eyes. But at least his office felt back to normal. No pretty blue-eyed strawberry blonde, tempting him to talk, to laugh, to like her.

He'd never wanted anything the way he wanted her. But they were wrong for each other. And it was *her* he was protecting from the pain that would result if they tried a relationship and it failed. She'd been through enough in her life without him putting her through something else.

By noon, the sounds of the silence of his office began to close in on him, but, luckily, he had a lunch out with Elias and Ricky to discuss the details of a new ad campaign created by the ad firm Tucker had hired.

Rick and Elias rose as he approached the table and so did the pretty blonde seated by Elias.

"Melinda Fornwalt, this is Tucker Engle."

She smiled and shook his hand. Painted up the way Maria usually was, Melinda might be pretty but since working with Vivi he sort of liked women with less makeup. Or maybe natural beauty?

"So this is Tucker Engle? The guy who made you rich."

Tucker held back a smile. Her voice and manners screamed socialite, somebody who lived the life of charities and theatre and loved it. He suspected Ricky had brought her on board to give the company the touch of class it was lacking.

"Yes and no. I paid to get controlling interest in their company but they were the ones with the idea. They made themselves rich."

She sat and the men sat.

"Still, you're quite the entrepreneur."

He removed his napkin. "Not really. My forte is buying existing companies. I'm more like a renovator than a carpenter."

She laughed. "Not just handsome and smart, you're funny, too."

His eyes narrowed. Was she coming on to him? She might be the kind of woman he typically dated, but for some reason or another, her flirting made him uneasy. No. Not uneasy. He didn't like it. At all.

"I'm sorry. I didn't catch your position with the company."

Elias cleared his throat. "She's not really with the company. She's with me."

He almost said, "And you tolerate her flirting with other men?" But he stopped himself if only to keep the situation civil. Unfortunately, as quickly as he thought that, he also imagined Vivi rolling her eyes about Melinda dating Elias and flirting with Tucker. And being correct. The woman was after Elias's money. That is, if she couldn't catch a bigger fish while going out with Elias.

He caught Ricky's gaze. "I'm guessing that means we won't be discussing the ad campaign you received."

Ricky shook his head as if to say he didn't know what was going on, but Elias blanched. "We can still talk about it."

"I never discuss business in front of people who don't have a financial interest in the project." He rose. "In fact, since we have to reschedule anyway, I think I'll go back to my office."

As soon as he was out on the street, he was sorry. Not only did he not want to go back to the overly keen Ward, but he was hungry. The scents of food beckoned but the one that caused him to stop came from the Chinese restaurant.

The last time he'd eaten Chinese, he'd been with Vivi's family. It had been a strange lunch, but he kept remembering how embarrassed Vivi had been. If there was one thing Vivi wasn't, it was a gold digger.

He shook his head. She was so determined to prove herself. So honest. So much fun. And that kiss in Italy had knocked him for a loop.

He didn't want to miss her, but he did. And not because Ward Bancroft was hard to work with. Because he liked Vivi—Olivia.

Just remembering her telling him to call her Olivia, caused his heart to jolt. He liked who he was with her. He especially liked talking to her. Honestly talking to her. And he'd sent her thousands of miles away.

The grassy fields of Italy relaxed Vivi, but working with Patrice and Antonio invigorated her. Even though the pair argued constantly, Vivi always seemed to be able to see a compromise position. They got more work done in two days than Patrice and Antonio had managed in the two weeks she'd been gone.

After a fattening supper of homemade butternut squash ravioli and two hours playing rummy with Constanzo, she took a long, hot shower and shimmied into a pair of pajamas, ready for sleep.

But as she tucked the covers to her chin and closed her eyes, the company cell phone rang. Tucker had given it to her in the last seconds before she left the office to pack for her trip. He'd said he didn't want to lose this deal and she was to call him if anything changed or if she needed help.

She didn't need help…but maybe he needed her?

Or maybe he just missed her?

Her heart skipped a beat. Two days out of each other's company and she'd missed him. Was it so unbelievable to think he might have missed her?

She grabbed the phone and said, "Hello."

"I think my new assistant wants my life."

Though his voice was serious and maybe even a tad desperate, she couldn't help it. She laughed.

"The little snot even dresses like me."

She sat up, made herself comfortable against the headboard. She could have taken him to task for not speaking to her in the weeks before Constanzo called her back to Italy. She could have reminded him he'd told her he didn't want to get personal because he couldn't be the man she wanted. She could have asked him if he really thought she could just drop her hurt feelings and talk to him now as if nothing had happened.

But she didn't. His life had been difficult, and maybe she needed to cut him some slack, give him some time to work out how he felt.

"You always told me you didn't care what I dressed like as long as I could do the job."

"He does everything too fast."

"And you're afraid he's missing things?"

"Absolutely." He groaned. "That's his word.

Absolutely. I ask for a report, he says, absolutely. I ask for coffee, he says absolutely."

"He's driving you nuts."

"He truly is."

"Want some advice?"

"It's why I called."

Her lips lifted into a happy smile. He trusted her. That's why he'd told her the little snippet of his past on spaghetti night. That's why he'd sent her to Italy without him. He might not *want* to like and trust her but he did. He'd come to a problem he couldn't solve and he'd turned to her.

"Call him in and tell him to relax. Or do what you did with me. Take him to a meeting. Make sure he knows he's to be seen and not heard. Remind him that a good assistant is nearly invisible."

"I didn't tell you that." His voice had calmed, almost warmed.

She settled more deeply into her pillow. Maybe he really had missed her, too? Or maybe it was just easier talking long distance? "Not in those words. But after the signing you told me that you appreciated that I hadn't said anything."

"And you extrapolated the rest?"

She thought about that. "Yeah, I guess."

"That's why you're good with people. You don't just read between the lines, you read the right subtext between the lines." He paused only slightly before he said, "How's Antonio?"

"I don't think Antonio is the problem. I think

it's Patrice. She likes schedules and timetables. Antonio sort of marches to his own drummer."

"Have you gotten him to put on a shirt?"

She laughed. "He always wears a shirt now."

"Yeah, but is it buttoned?"

The tone of his voice sent a little jolt of hope to her lonely heart. "Are you jealous?"

"No. More like confused. Wondering if I'd get better deals if I stopped wearing ties and showed off a little chest hair."

She laughed with delight and Tucker settled more comfortably into his seat in the limo. He'd missed her terribly. It was wrong, and calling her probably wasn't fair to her, but he'd needed to hear her voice. He'd happily jumped on the excuse of needing advice about his new assistant.

"Seriously, how's it going over there?"

"Actually it's going very well. Antonio considers Constanzo his benefactor and by default a mentor. He seems to like and trust him. I'd say we could tell him now that Constanzo's his dad, except I don't want to screw up his showing."

"I agree. That show needs to go well."

"Especially since Antonio's invested in it. This isn't just his career. Painting is his life. I want to tread lightly here. I want to do this right."

The limo pulled up to Tucker's building. "Then we'll do it right." Maurice opened the door. "Trust your gut, Miss Prentiss. So far you seem to be doing very well."

He stepped out onto the street and inhaled the fresh New York City air after a rain storm. The empty, hollow feeling he'd been carrying around in his gut since she'd left had disappeared. He'd gotten the advice he'd wanted about his new assistant and received an update on her circumstances. There was nothing more to say.

"Good night, Miss Prentiss."

He disconnected the call and headed to the penthouse of his Park Avenue apartment. The quiet of the elevator rattled through him, reminding him again that in his sixties he'd be Constanzo Bartulocci.

When the doors opened on his slick white, black and chrome apartment, the silence was deafening. He unexpectedly wished he'd kept Olivia on the phone for another ten minutes, at least until he had a drink in his hand and the sports channel on TV. But that was foolish. Stupid. He couldn't have her. As he'd told her, he couldn't be what she wanted. And he was going to have to control this.

Tomorrow. For tonight, he was glad he'd called. Glad she'd made him laugh. Glad she was doing well.

The next day, he did as Olivia had suggested. He took Ward Bancroft to a lunch meeting. He told him it was not his job to talk, but to be available to find information and to observe. At the meeting, the kid was so quiet one wouldn't have even known he was there.

In the limo on the way back, Tucker complimented him on a job well done and Ward virtually glowed.

Every assignment he gave him that afternoon
was completed with the utmost care, and he had
a much more professional tone with visitors.

Of course, most of his visitors had liked Olivia better, but that was beside the point. He had
companies to run, jobs to be done, investments
to be investigated. He and his assistant were not
there to have fun.

Still, riding up the elevator to the penthouse
that night, he pulled out his cell and speed-di-
aled Olivia.

"Hello."

"You sound freshly showered."

"Now how would you know that?"

He smiled shrewdly. He wasn't the only one
who could handle people. "I don't. I took a wild
guess and led you into a statement that confirmed
it. *That's* how I deal with people."

"I prefer my direct approach."

"I sort of like being sneaky."

"No kidding."

The elevator ride wasn't interminable. The
doors opening on his penthouse apartment didn't
feel like the boring, silent gates of hell yawning
open before him. He slid out of his jacket and
walked to the bar.

"I did what you suggested with Mr. Bancroft and today he was as sharp as a brand-new pencil."

"That's great."

After pouring two fingers of Scotch, he fell to a furry white chaise. He put his feet up. Put his shoulders back. Sipped his favorite malt liquor and savored.

"We work like a well-oiled machine. He knows the right questions to ask. He doesn't ask stupid things. I think I've found a keeper."

His happiness was met with resounding silence and he stared at the phone for a few seconds before she said, "That's really good for him. And you. I guess."

"Miss Prentiss, you've done nothing but whine about wanting to be in Accounting since the day I dragged you kicking and screaming out of HR. Why would the news that I found someone who fits the position upset you?"

"Nobody wants to be so easily replaced, Tucker."

"You haven't really been replaced. Technically, you've moved on."

"To become a babysitter?"

"To become a manager. A business manager for Antonio."

"I hardly feel like a business manager."

"What do you think mangers do? They solve goofy nitpicky problems."

Her cautiously optimistic voice tiptoed across the Atlantic to him. "So I'm a manager?"

"And you could suggest to Constanzo that he hire you permanently for his son."

Her breath hissed over the phone. "Are you trying to get rid of me *completely?*"

"No." His own breath stumbled. What *was* he doing? "I just…It's just… Well, some people are made to be assistants and some people are meant to be…more."

"You're telling me I'm made to be more?"

"Of course, you're meant to be more. Look at you. In a few weeks, you've gone from working for the head of your company to jet-setting around the globe and infiltrating the art world." He paused, let his ice clink around the walls of his glass. "Olivia, have you ever asked yourself what *you* wanted?"

"I want to be a success."

"And you believed an accounting degree was the best way to get there?"

"Can't run a company if you don't know the basics of the numbers behind it."

"So you want to run your own company?"

She hesitated. "I guess…someday."

"You've shown a talent for being able to get people to do what you want them to do. That's your service…or your stock-in-trade. Now you merely have to figure out who your customer base would be. Then you have to market yourself."

He finished his drink. "Think it through tonight and I'll call you tomorrow. We'll make some decisions."

He hung up the phone and walked back down the hall to his big empty master suite with the equally big and equally empty master bathroom. But tonight, he didn't notice those. Though his home was empty, inside he was full, busy, thinking about Olivia. Her talent. Her skills. How he could help her become the person she wanted to be.

The next day, as she sweet-talked Antonio and persuaded Patrice, Vivi thought about what Tucker had said about becoming a business manager. But she thought more about the fact that he was back to speaking to her casually, as if they were friends.

All day she wondered what she'd say to him. As she signed for deliveries, debated placement with Patrice, soothed Antonio and constantly updated Constanzo, she thought about the job—what she was really doing for Antonio.

When Tucker called that night, after she'd showered, slid into her very best pajamas and snuggled into her pillow, she said, "I think I'm actually a mother."

He laughed.

"Seriously. Constanzo's like the big lovable dad. Patrice is the grouchy middle daughter who wants everything her own way and Antonio's the spoiled baby boy."

"Managers are a lot like mothers—babysitters—what have you, because there are some people who need a 'career' mother. You, as a business, have to find a focus so you learn that world and how to navigate in it."

"Makes sense."

"Do you want to manage artists like Antonio? Or singers? Or rock bands?"

"Is this how you did it?"

"Did what?"

"Decided what to do with your life?"

He got more comfortable on his bed. Tonight he'd showered and put on silky navy blue pajama bottoms before he'd called her. He wasn't entirely sure why he'd left off the top, except he knew it had something to do with Antonio, even though she couldn't see his chest over the phone—damn. They should be video calling! He had two fingers of Scotch on ice and his day had gone fairly well.

Yet he'd still looked forward to this call like a kid at Christmas.

He winced. All but two of his Christmases had been abysmal.

The reminder brought him back to reality. He wasn't supposed to like her. He was helping find her place in the world as a way to repay her for her help with Antonio. "My decisions about what to do with my life had more to do with getting a roof over my head and keeping food in my stomach."

"Was it bad?"

He hesitated. For as much as he didn't want *anybody* to know this part of his life, didn't want anybody to pity him, had been unable to talk about it with her at Constanzo's, he suddenly had an uncontrollable desire to tell her. Probably because they were on the phone and he couldn't see her face, her reactions, her pity.

"A person can sleep on a bench and go without supper and forget about it in a few days. But the feeling of being the only person in your world, having no mom, no dad, no brothers, no sisters... That doesn't ever go away."

"I have a great family."

"Thanks for rubbing that in."

She laughed and for some reason or another, in his mind's eye, he pictured her tucking her feet beneath a soft pink robe as she snuggled into her pillow. "No, silly. I'm suggesting you spend time with them."

"So I can see how the other half lives?"

"So you can see that you'd blend in. My dad's the easiest person in the world to become friends with." She paused. "If you golf. Do you golf?"

Confusion sprang up inside him. How would it feel to be part of her family? "I've made some of my best deals on the golf course."

"Thank God. And my mother loves everybody.

Though Cindy can be a pain in the butt like Patrice."

"Ah, thus the comparison to the bossy sister."

"And Billy's the spoiled little brother like Antonio. Now that you know all that, you'll fit right in. You can come to our house for every Christmas, Thanksgiving and Easter dinner for the rest of your life."

His heart stuttered. He'd received other invitations, of course. A wealthy man never spent a holiday alone unless he wanted to. But the picture that formed in his head warmed him. He could see himself going into Olivia's home, armed with gifts, accepting hugs from her crazy family and rubbing his hands in anticipation over a tray of fresh snickerdoodle cookies.

He shook his head to clear it. It was one thing to wish for a second that he belonged, quite another to indulge the fantasy. It was time to get this conversation back to planet earth.

"And what happens after you get married? Your husband isn't going to want your ex-boss showing up every holiday."

"What if I marry you?"

The thought paralyzed him so quickly he felt like he'd vibrated to a stop.

"Marry me?"

"You're not completely unacceptable or hopeless. A few more lessons in communicating like a normal human being and I might actually like you."

Male pride surged. There was no way he'd let her get away with that. "You already like me."

"A tad."

"A tad?"

"Okay, more than a tad. But you like me, too."

It was another perfect opportunity to disabuse her of any romantic notions. Yet instead of forming words to correct her, he felt his own mouth forming the words he shouldn't say.

"A bit."

"Uh-huh. You keep telling yourself that. We like each other and you know it."

Though her presumptuousness should have annoyed him, her words settled over him like a soft blanket. She was bossy and nosy but usually right and he liked her. If he wasn't careful, she'd drag his entire life and all his secrets out of him one phone call at a time.

He changed the subject. "Did I tell you I found another company I might like to buy?"

"You find a new company every day. But in a few weeks you may be on the hook for about a billion bucks to buy out Constanzo. Do I have to put a lock on your checkbook?"

He laughed. "I'd just go to a bank and get a line of credit."

"You are a bad boy."

He laughed again, loving how normal she made

him feel. "I want you to know, Miss Prentiss, that whatever you decide to do with your talent, I'm going to fund it. We'll call you a start-up. You'll get capital. I'll lend you a few advisors for marketing. And this time next year you could be a superstar manager."

"Once again, it feels like you're trying to get rid of me."

"You wouldn't let me give you the bonus. And you may end up being the force that gets me Constanzo Bartulocci's fortune. I think I owe you."

"I like the sound of that."

He shook his head. "Good night, Miss Prentiss."

"Good night."

The next day when he called her, he immediately got them down to business. "I spoke with Constanzo today about hiring you to manage Antonio."

Her breath caught. "What?"

"You're in. You've already started. I'm funding you. You now have a client."

Instead of protesting that he was trying to get rid of her, she laughed. "I'm a company?"

"You are a company."

"Thanks."

No one word had ever split his heart the way her sincere thanks had. The feeling was like warm rain or a soft snowfall on Christmas morning.

Something you didn't even know you wanted until it was there.

He whispered, "You're welcome."

The phone line grew quiet and he suddenly wanted to tell her just how much he liked her. But he stopped himself. He wasn't sure either one of them was ready for that. But he couldn't deny that every day, every phone call, he wanted to tell her just a little bit more. And he knew that if he didn't stop calling her, one of these days the cat would be out of the bag.

"Just remember, you still work for me until after Antonio's show. Constanzo understands that until this whole process is done, you're an employee of Inferno."

She laughed. "I understand that I still work for you. I remember that my primary mission is to make sure this show goes well so we can tell Antonio that Constanzo is his father."

"Good."

The line grew quiet again and fear suddenly engulfed him. Now that she had a business, his support and a client, what if she didn't want *him* anymore? Maybe in giving her a soft place to land he'd given her a way out. He wasn't exactly the easiest guy to love. She could take his money and run now.

"Did I ever tell you about the time my mom bought me a puppy for Christmas?"

That brought him up short. Confused, he said, "No."

"Well, if I tell you that story, you have to tell me one, too."

Even as relief poured through him, another kind of fear raced in behind it. With every step of honesty they took, they got a step closer to discovering the truth. Did they belong together? Were they good for each other? Or was he just so tired of being alone he was clinging to the first person with whom he could be honest?

He didn't know. But he did know she made him laugh, made him feel whole.

"You remember the story about the video game. My stories might start happy but they end miserably."

Ignoring that, she broke into a long story about a puppy bought for her one Christmas that had fallen in love with her dad instead of her. "To really understand the story you have to remember my dad is bald."

"I remember."

"So one morning my mom wakes up and the dog is sleeping on my dad's pillow, right above his head and it looked like he had hair. She screamed bloody murder until she realized it was just the dog."

Tucker laughed. "That's the stupidest thing I've ever heard."

"Yeah, my family can be pretty silly." She paused a second. "Now your turn."

"Okay." It had taken him the length of her entire story, but he'd finally remembered something he could tell her. "In second grade, I won my first spelling bee."

"First?"

"I was champ every year after that. No matter where I lived or what school I went to, I won my division of that spelling bee."

"So that was the beginning of your overachieving."

He sniffed a laugh. "Yeah. I guess."

The warmth of feeling normal flowed through him again, and from that moment on, he knew he'd call her every night.

Though he didn't have a clue in hell where they'd end up, he was fairly certain one of them or both of them was going to get hurt.

CHAPTER TWELVE

THE DOORBELL AT CONSTANZO'S house rang for the fiftieth time the morning of Antonio's opening and Vivi rushed to get it. Busy with preparations for the elaborate party after the gallery doors closed, the staff had better things to do than sign for deliveries.

The uniformed man handed her a box and a clipboard and pen. She juggled them, until Maria Bartulocci appeared at her side. Not one to let an enormous party given by her incredibly wealthy uncle occur without her input, Maria had arrived two days before and she'd taken over the planning.

"Here. I will help."

Handing the box to Maria, Vivi scanned the delivery information and realized the box was for her. She signed the sheet, gave it back to the deliveryman and closed the door.

"It's for me."

Maria held it up as if weighing it. "Too heavy to be flowers."

She grabbed the card and ripped it open.

We can't have the prettiest girl there in anything but the best. Tucker.

Maria rolled her eyes. "My God, he's a sap."

But Vivi's heart about exploded in her chest. Not because he'd sent her a dress, but because he wasn't running from what was happening between them. Something real. Some wonderful. Their nighttime chats had become longer and more personal. They'd stopped talking like a boss and assistant and begun talking like friends, but she could feel there was something more behind it.

Still, she wasn't about to tell Maria that.

"He knows I'm poor. I'd told him I'd have to squeeze out a few hours to go into town today to find something to wear." Because she desperately wanted to be beautiful for him. To feel like the woman he saw when he looked at her. "This is his way of being a good boss, making sure I have everything I need for my job."

Maria laughed and batted her hand as she led Vivi up the stairs. "He likes you. Not like he would like me—for fun. He likes you for you." She shook her head. "I don't want that. But you do."

"I do." Vivi couldn't deny that. She wanted their chats to cross the line from friendship into relationship. And if she let herself, she could almost believe this dress was Tucker's way of doing that.

"Then we'll have fun with this."

They took the big box down the hall to Vivi's lilac-and-white bedroom. The second she set it on the bed, Maria pulled the ribbon to unravel the bow. Vivi lifted the lid.

Inside was a raspberry-colored chiffon dress.

A laugh escaped. Raspberry was the color of the bathing suit she'd worn their first day in Italy.

Something soft and warm surrounded her heart. He was telling her he remembered details, maybe everything that had happened between them.

Maria eyed her askance. "What?"

She wasn't about to tell Maria this either. Especially if she was reading all the signals wrong. Plus, this wasn't something she felt like sharing. She just wanted to hug the information to herself. Hug the dress to herself. Be a simple, silly girl falling in love.

But she couldn't. She had absolutely no idea how Tucker felt about her.

She turned to Maria with a short smile. "Nothing. I just love the dress." She pulled it out of the box. "Do you think it will fit?"

"I think a man like Tucker knows his way around a woman's curves."

Maria's snarky comment barely registered as she fought the urge to hug the dress. She'd found a calling. Something that gave her a sense of self-worth that went beyond proving herself to a bunch of people in Starlight, Kentucky, who no longer mattered. She was on the global stage, helping

one of the most talented new artists in the *world*
start his career.

And Tucker liked her.

She knew he did. She didn't want to deny herself the pleasure of believing it.

"So we play with your hair and makeup until
we get it perfect," Maria said, but Vivi stepped
away from her.

"I thought you were helping arrange the pool
area for tonight's party."

"They will be fine without me."

"No," Vivi said, laying the dress across the bed.
She slipped off her T-shirt and slid out of her
jeans. "Once we make sure this puppy fits, we're
both going back to work."

"You are no fun, Vivi."

"No. I keep my promises, Maria. And as long
as I'm working with Antonio and you're anywhere
near Antonio, you're going to keep your promises
to him, too."

Vivi slipped into the dress, which fit perfectly.
Strapless, it caressed her breasts and torso to the
waist where it belled out into a frothy skirt that
stopped three inches above the knee.

The dress fit so perfectly Vivi shivered. When
had he studied her so well, so often?

"I have a necklace that would look wonderful
with that dress," Maria said, racing out the door.
In two minutes she was back, holding a thin chain
with a simple round ruby.

Vivi gasped. "I couldn't!"

"Please," Maria scoffed. "I got this from a man I now hate. If you lost it, it would be a favor."

Vivi shook her head. "You're bad."

"I am terrible," Maria happily agreed as she secured the necklace on Vivi and turned her to face the mirror.

Vivi touched it reverently. "It does look wonderful."

"*Sì.* You will wear this tonight." She unclasped the necklace and set it on the dresser for Vivi to find that evening. Then she casually ran her finger along the clean wooden vanity top, as if unconcerned. "Why do you have this interest in Antonio? If you like Tucker, why do you follow Antonio around like a little dog?"

"Because Constanzo wants me to." She wouldn't tell her that Tucker had already talked to Constanzo about making this a full-time job. Sweet and generous as she could be sometimes, Maria had a hard side, a scary side. "And my boss wants to do whatever pleases your uncle. No matter how much fun this seems to be, the bottom line is I still work for Inferno and I do whatever Tucker tells me."

Maria said, "Uh-huh," but Vivi got a bad feeling. No longer interested in Vivi or her dress, Maria flitted out of the room. Vivi removed the dress and reverently laid it across the bed. Tonight she would look perfect for him.

* * *

Tucker didn't time his arrival to be so close to the actual show opening, but delays had caused him to leave late enough that he'd changed into his tux on his plane and didn't bother going to Constanzo's. He took the limo directly to Patrice's villa gallery.

White lights had been strung across the second-floor balcony and the leafy trees that lined the cobblestone walk that led to the front door. With fifteen minutes to spare before the actual opening, he strode up the walk and slipped in the front door.

His favorite Antonio painting—blue wildflowers in the sea of green grass beneath a pale blue sky—sat on an easel in the center of the foyer, teasing attendees with a sample of his talent. A glance into the rooms on the right and the left showed the elaborate displays of more of Antonio's work.

He heard the clack, clack, click of shoes on marble and he spun toward the sound, but all he saw was a swatch of pink.

That was the dress.

After two weeks of talking on the phone, growing closer and closer, he was finally going to see her.

His heart racing, he headed in the direction that he'd seen the blur of pink, but by the time he reached the room, she was gone. He stood in the area filled with Antonio's paintings as catering staff brought trays of appetizers to the long thin tables lining the walls.

Shoving his hands into his pockets, he glanced around. What was he doing? He never, ever chased a woman—

But he caught a glimpse of the pink dress again and that crazy combination of warmth and excitement tightened his chest, warmed his blood. He couldn't resist this any more than he could hold back a rising tide.

"Olivia! Vivi!"

She stopped.

As she turned to face him, her lips lifted slowly. Her eyes warmed. His heart stumbled and he realized he'd been waiting two long weeks to see that smile.

"I'm so glad you're here."

So was he. The happiness that rose inside him was so intense it couldn't even be described.

"Everything's falling apart."

His joy deflated like a popped balloon. "You want me here because everything's falling apart?"

She winced. "Yes."

It wasn't exactly what a man wanted to hear when he hadn't seen the woman he desired in two weeks. But he told himself not to panic. First, she was under a lot of pressure. Second, it was good to hear she needed him. Really good. She could be so self-sufficient, especially with Antonio, that it was reassuring that she turned to him.

He put his hands on her bare shoulders to steady her. The velvet smoothness of her skin shuddered through him but he held her a few inches away so he could take in the vision she made in the frothy dress. Tall and lean, with graceful arms and shapely legs, she wore the little pink creation as if it were made for her. Her thick strawberry blonde hair had been caught up in a curly creation that allowed tendrils of hair to tickle her neck and tease his imagination. Makeup enhanced her blue eyes. The sprinkle of gloss on her lips tempted him to kiss her.

He couldn't kiss her, not publicly, not when he wasn't entirely sure what was happening between them. But even if the world was crumbling around them, he needed to acknowledge that she was the prettiest thing he'd ever seen.

"You're beautiful."

Her eyes lit. The corners of her lips kicked upward. And his Vivi was back. "What? This old thing?"

"Hey, that old thing cost a bundle."

"And I appreciate that you thought of me. I was just about to steal a minute away from the chaos and go into town to find something to wear when this arrived." She stood on her tiptoes and kissed his cheek. "You're the best boss ever."

Frustration knotted in his chest. He wanted a

kiss, a real kiss, for his thoughtfulness, and she had bussed his cheek. Still, he was the one who needed to keep their relationship simple until he figured out what he really wanted.

"And I'll pay you back."

"You can't pay me back." The words were out before he could stop them. He'd already decided to tell her the dress cost five hundred dollars, rather than the five thousand he'd spent. But his damned male pride swooped in and stole those words. He longed to be allowed to spoil her. But she wouldn't let him. And his own fears stopped him, too.

Once, just once, he wanted to relax and let go. Do what he wanted, just because he wanted to.

He softened his voice. "I won't take your money if you try to pay me back."

She smoothed her hand across the soft chiffon. "It's too much."

"For whom? Do you realize what's exorbitant to you is like pocket change to me?"

Her gaze snapped up. "So this is pocket change?"

"Essentially. But it was also my way of celebrating your success. Other people send champagne. I sent a dress."

Their eyes met and temptation tugged at him again. He wanted a kiss so bad his chest hurt from it. But life wasn't always fair or easy. He wished he could look into those big blue eyes and know everything would be okay if they crossed the line from friends to lovers. But he couldn't and neither could she.

As if disappointed, she stepped back, wringing her hands. "Don't celebrate too soon. Maria knows something is up."

"And?"

"And you do know Maria, right? She's a busybody."

"We can handle her."

"You think? She expected to inherit Uncle Constanzo's wealth…or at least to live off the gravy train for the rest of her life. With a son, an heir, in the way…do you really think she's going to take this calmly?"

She stopped suddenly. Her lips lifted into a smile of pure pleasure. As if only now really seeing him, she said, "Wow. Look at you."

He smiled.

"You look fantastic."

"I do, don't I?" A man didn't get to thirty-four, and have the brain to acquire wealth that exceeded the gross national product of most small countries, without knowing his assets.

Her gaze dipped. "A little vain tonight?"

"It's hardly vain when it's the truth." He stepped closer, slid his arm around her waist, forced her gaze to his. Her eyes met his with a longing that mirrored the feeling churning in his gut. He knew this was risky or maybe too soon. But the need to touch her simply overwhelmed him.

"Besides, we look good together. Very good."

"Tucker!" Maria's voice echoed along the high ceilings of the villa entrance.

He released Vivi and spun around. Maria raced toward him. She caught his upper arms and planted a kiss on each cheek. "So are you going to tell me what's really going on here?"

He peeled her hands off his upper arms and turned her around. "Go fix your lipstick. Olivia and I have work to do."

When she was gone, Tucker sighed heavily. "We've got to get Constanzo to tell Antonio tonight. This can't wait till morning."

She bit her lower lip. "It has to be after the show. Antonio can't take that kind of surprise before his big moment."

"Okay. How about after the show but before the party at his house? We'll get them in the same limo and not let anyone else in."

"Okay."

"Which means we have to warn Constanzo that he'd better prepare his speech for Antonio, and to watch out for Maria."

She nodded.

He caught her hand. "Let's go find him now."

They searched the first floor of the gallery and found him with Antonio who looked ready to throw up.

"Doors open in ten minutes," Vivi reminded Antonio. He looked amazing in his black tuxedo but not as good as Tucker. Tucker wore formal attire as if he'd been born to it, but she knew he hadn't been. There was so much about him that was special, intriguing, and she suspected she was one of only a few people he trusted with his secrets. "But you don't have to show up right away unless you want to. If I were you, I'd give people a chance to look around, then you could kind of slide into the crowd and introduce yourself."

"You will be with me?"

She glanced at Tucker. She wanted to be with *him*. She wanted to walk the gallery with him and tell him every silly nitpicky story of how each displayed painting had been chosen. How Antonio and Patrice had argued over placement. How she'd intervened and stopped fight after fight.

Instead, she said, "I'll stay by your side all night if that's what you want."

He caught her hands, kissed the knuckles. "It's what I want."

Tucker said, "Super," as Constanzo nervously said "Great."

Vivi let go of Antonio's hands. "But for right now, why don't you go up to Patrice's apartment and just chill. Find a soccer game or something on TV. I'll come and get you a half hour after the doors have been opened."

Constanzo volunteered to walk upstairs with him, but Tucker caught his arm. "Vivi and I need to talk to you for a second."

He motioned Antonio to go on without him. "I'll be right behind you." When Antonio was gone, he faced Tucker. "You don't think it's a good idea for me to stay with my son when he so clearly needs me?"

"I think it's a great idea," Vivi said. "Especially since I think Maria is catching on."

"Catching on to what?"

"Catching on to the fact that there must be a reason you're going to all this trouble for Antonio," Tucker said.

Constanzo fell to an available chair.

Vivi stooped beside him. "She knows you too well. All along she's thought you were going overboard for this project. But today she came right out and asked what was going on."

"We think you need to tell Antonio before the party."

Constanzo's gaze shot to Tucker. "Here? At the showing?"

"How about in the limo on the way home?"

He nodded. "*Sì*. The party can be ruined. But the showing must be perfect."

The two floors of Patrice's villa quickly filled with art enthusiasts and Constanzo's friends. Guests spilled out in the gardens. Waiters wove through the crowd with champagne.

A half hour into the event, Vivi left Tucker and went to Patrice's apartment and retrieved Antonio. She guided him to Constanzo who took him from one circle of friends to the next. Seeing how confident Constanzo was with his guests, she could have stolen away at any time, but she'd made a promise to Antonio and she kept it. Still, she didn't stay on the sidelines. She was as much a part of this event, of Antonio's success at this event, as anyone. So she talked with Constanzo's guests, sipped champagne and in general made Antonio as comfortable as she could.

Tucker watched, growing more and more agitated. He wanted to be with her tonight. He'd missed her. Even though they'd talked every night, it wasn't enough. In fact, sometimes talking to her without seeing her had been torture.

He was here. She was here. They should be together. She shouldn't be with Antonio. She should be with him.

His mental temper tantrum stopped him. He wasn't just eager to see her. He wasn't just longing to see her. He was possessive. And being possessive was dangerous. Every person who'd ever come into his life had left him.

He did not want to be hurt again.

But with every second that ticked off the clock, and every move she made with Antonio from one crowd of art enthusiasts to the next, his heart beat a little harder, a little faster. If this was jealousy he hated it. And if this was jealousy didn't that mean that he felt a little more for Olivia than he'd let himself believe?

Still, could he trust her with his heart? Trust her never to leave?

As the night wound down and guests began heading to Constanzo's, he watched Olivia commandeer a limo for Constanzo and Antonio. She kissed Antonio's cheek. "Congratulations on a wonderful show. I'll be at the house as soon as everything is closed up here."

As Antonio climbed into the limo, she kissed Constanzo's cheek. "Good luck."

He sucked in a breath. "I will need it."

"No, you won't." She straightened his bow tie. "You'll tell him the truth. His mother came to you once and disappeared." She kissed his cheek again. "You can do this."

As Constanzo's limo pulled away and another drove up, she turned to walk into the gallery.

Tucker glanced back at Olivia and then at the limo. If he timed this right, he could wheedle the last limo for himself and Olivia. He could finally have the ten minutes of peace and privacy he'd wanted since they'd arrived.

He opened the limo door slowly enough that the first couple slid in just as the second couple walked toward the limo door. He managed to pair couple after couple into limos until, exactly as he wanted, a limo pulled up as Olivia walked toward him. She carried the raspberry-colored wrap that matched her dress in one hand and a small purse in the other.

He opened the door for her with a smile. She accepted his courtesy with a nod and her own smile, and slid inside. He slid in beside her.

"I thought I'd missed you while I was in New York, but that was nothing compared to the torture of watching you all night."

"Watching me was torture?"

He laughed. "Watching you was fun, but I didn't want to watch you. I wanted to kiss you."

Her eyes widened. "Really?"

He drifted closer. "Yes. I can't say for sure you'll never leave me. I can't say for sure what I feel for you is love. But I do know I can't ignore what I feel. I wanted you desperately."

Olivia's eyes widened. "Really?"

"Really?" He paused, realizing his mistake. The last man she'd been involved with had attacked her. He hadn't even thought of that in weeks. Hadn't taken that into consideration when he thought about the possibility of loving her.

What if she wasn't ready?

CHAPTER THIRTEEN

ON THE DRIVE TO CONSTANZO'S, Tucker turned the conversation to Antonio's showing. Olivia didn't know whether to breathe a sigh of relief or yell at herself. She'd waited two weeks to see him and now suddenly she was afraid?

He'd never hurt her the way Cord had, but that was because he could hurt her in a worse way. She loved him. And he confided in her, got her jobs, bought her dresses. None of which meant he loved her. For all she knew, he wanted sex. And the way she felt tonight, she'd be a very easy target. But what would happen in the morning?

When they arrived, he got out of the limo and turned around to help Olivia out. She smiled, trying not to be panicky.

He tapped her nose affectionately. "Let's find Constanzo."

Then he took her hand and her heart stuttered. Sweet and loving, the gesture soothed her jumping nerves. He wasn't a guy she had to be afraid of. She loved him. Trusted him.

They found Constanzo on the patio by the pool beside Antonio as if holding court.

Careful not to disturb the artist or his group of admirers, she pulled Constanzo away from the small crowd. "How did it go?"

He laughed. "Antonio was a bit surprised." He winced. "Shocked actually, but we agreed to work this out."

She squeezed his forearm. "That's so exciting."

He nodded. "And I have you to thank." He faced Tucker. "And you. It looks like we'll be in some heavy-duty negotiation starting tomorrow."

Tucker shook his hand. "I look forward to it."

With that, Constanzo rejoined his son. Antonio turned to him with a smile and Vivi's heart melted. They had done it.

Tucker faced Olivia. "So."

She stepped toward him. "So?"

"I think we're free."

She ran her hand down his lapels. With things settled with Constanzo, and because Tucker had held her hand, hadn't kissed her, hadn't rushed her, everything suddenly felt okay. She loved this man, and she believed in her heart of hearts he loved her. She could not be a coward.

"You're about to start the biggest negotiations of your life. That's not freedom. That's work."

"Yeah. But I can do these negotiations in my sleep." He grinned. "I kinda owe this to you."

"You bet you do."

He slid his hands to her waist. "I could think of about thirty ways I could repay you."

Need sizzled through her. She'd never been more ready or more afraid. But she knew she had to do this. Conquer her fears. Be with the man she loved. "You're inventive."

"I like to think so." For Tucker, everything suddenly seemed easy, right, and he didn't care that they were in a crowd. He dipped his head and kissed her. The kiss was slow and sweet, like nothing he'd ever experienced. It wasn't just physical. It was personal, emotional, intimate—if only because she knew him. And he knew her. He'd never realized two serious, broken people could be so playful, so happy. And that's what he really owed to Olivia. His soul.

Her purse began to play out a lively beat. She pulled away, opening it. "It's the cell phone you gave me." She caught his gaze. "I thought only you had that number."

"It's company property. Human Resources has it, too."

She rummaged to find the phone. "What could they want?"

Before she could get it out of her purse the call went to voice mail, but a few seconds later her phone buzzed with a text.

Looking over her shoulder, Tucker saw it was from her mom.

Call me. Emergency.

She immediately punched a number into the cell phone.

"Mom?"

Tucker watched Vivi's face fall as she listened to her mother and his heart kicked against his ribs.

"What kind of accident?"

Filled with a fear he'd never experienced, Tucker stood impotently, waiting. When she disconnected the call, her eyes glistened with tears.

"What happened?"

"My sister was driving in the rain, a deer ran out in front of her and when she swerved to miss it, she hit a tree."

"Oh, my God."

"My mom said they aren't sure how bad it is. Cindy's in surgery right now—" Her lips trembled. She pressed her fingers to them. "I have to go home."

He pulled Vivi against him with one arm, then retrieved his cell phone from his pocket and hit a speed-dial number. "Jonah, get the plane ready. File a flight plan for the airport closest to Starlight, Kentucky. Have a car ready for us when we land."

Huddled into his shoulder she said, "I don't want to take your plane. You might need it while you're here."

"You're not taking my plane. *We're* taking my plane."

She pulled away so she could look at him. "You're coming with me?"

"Yes." Though it astounded him, he couldn't let her go alone. He didn't have a sister or a brother to be able to relate to her feelings, but maybe that was the point. Knowing how priceless siblings could be, he couldn't let her suffer the thought of losing one of them alone.

With an explanation to Constanzo, they left the party as unobtrusively as possible. Exhausted from the long weeks she'd had with Antonio, Vivi fell asleep on the flight. Tucker found her a blanket and pillow, marveling at how different this trip was from their first flight to Italy. With so much work to do for his negotiations with Constanzo, he could have gone back to his makeshift desk. Instead, he sat on the seat beside her, letting her lean against him while she slept.

When they landed in Kentucky, he woke her.

"Where are we?"

"If my calculations are correct we're about two hours away from your home." He clicked a few buttons on his smart phone. "And there is no limo service here so Jonah rented a car for us."

They got out of the plane at the small public airport. There was only one rental car agency. When he walked up to the counter, he gave them a credit card, signed a few forms and they presented him with keys.

Still wearing her frothy pink dress, Olivia drew all kinds of strange looks from passersby. Behind her in his tux, he got his fair share of odd glances, too.

"We should probably find Jonah, get our bags and change."

"I don't want to waste time."

Tucker caught her by the shoulders. "This isn't a waste of time. We need to get into comfortable clothes. We need to get something to eat. Maybe a bottle of water. We have a two-hour drive ahead of us. Call your mom. See how things are going. If there's no news, we have plenty of time to change."

She closed her eyes. "I'm afraid to."

"You? Olivia 'Vivi' Prentiss? A woman who yelled at her boss? You're afraid?"

"I never yelled at you. I just made a few points strongly. And this is different. This is my sister. I don't want to talk on the phone. I need to be there."

He turned her in the direction of the door where they'd pick up their rental car. "If you're okay, I'm okay. But we are stopping somewhere for water."

She was out the door before he'd even said water. He ran after her to find Jonah just outside the door, holding their bags. He located their rental car, Jonah tucked the luggage in the trunk and he and Vivi slid into the front seat.

Before they left, he used his phone's GPS to find the best route to the hospital and they drove away from the municipal airport.

He tried to think of something hopeful to say, but nothing came to mind. He almost said, "Everything's going to be fine," but he didn't know that it was. He considered telling her to hang in there, but that sounded stupid.

He glanced over at her. She leaned back against the headrest, her eyes closed in misery, her usually happy face drawn in grim lines. Pain sliced through his heart. He couldn't stand to see her this way.

"Please call your mom." The words came up from the deepest part of him. "For all we know, there could be good news."

She opened her eyes slowly and retrieved the cell phone from her purse. She punched in the numbers. Her voice wobbled when she said, "Mom?"

There was a pause that filled the car with reverent silence. Finally she said, "How she can still be in surgery? That's over eight hours now."

She quieted again as her mother spoke. Tears filled her eyes. And he wanted to kick himself for insisting she call.

"So they're saying the surgery could go on for twelve hours? Four more hours?"

Another pause.

"We're on our way. Tucker's driving. There's nothing to worry about."

Her little bit of confidence in his driving at least gave him the feeling he was doing something. He tried twice to get her to talk. Once about Antonio. Once about how he'd negotiate with Constanzo. But she barely listened. She didn't care. And he didn't blame her.

When they finally made it to the hospital, he parked the car and held on to her elbow as she tried to frantically race into the building. They stopped at the information desk and were told the number of the floor for the surgical waiting room. They stayed quiet as they rode the elevator.

As the doors opened, she raced out. He followed at a slower pace. He'd been inept in the car. Clueless about what to say. He could only imagine how he'd boggle things if he tried to talk to her family.

He stepped into the waiting room in time to see her in a group hug with her mom and dad and younger brother. Her parents wept as her brother tried to keep a stiff upper lip. And Vivi, his Olivia, just fell apart.

Total uselessness rattled through him. He knew nothing about families, knew nothing about this kind of loss, had no idea what to say or do.

After what felt like forever, she pulled away from the group. She faced him, her eyes red rimmed, her nose runny and his heart broke again as impotence filled him. Shaming him. Scaring him.

What the hell did a person say or do at a time like this?

"Mom, Dad, Billy…" Her breath shuddered in and out, a remnant of her crying. "You remember my boss, Tucker Engle."

Though it felt incredibly odd to be called her boss, he stepped forward to shake her dad's hand.

Vivi sniffed a laugh. "I think right now I need that bottle of water you offered me at the airport."

"Okay, one water. Would anyone else like anything?"

Her mother said, "I wouldn't mind a coffee."

Her dad ran his hand along the back of his neck. "Coffee would be good for me, too."

Billy said, "I'll take a soda." He moved away from the group. "But I'll also show you the way to the cafeteria. Coffee from the vending machines is worthless."

As they walked out the door, he nearly breathed a sigh of relief, not sure if he was glad to be getting her parents decent coffee, or glad to be getting out of the room.

"So you brought Vivi the whole way from Italy."

"It's kind of easy when you have a private plane."

Billy snorted. "I guess." He paused, caught Tucker's gaze. "You know, my sister really likes you."

Another wave of relief poured through him but on its heels came an odd sense that he'd never felt before. Olivia liked him in his world. Now, here they were in hers and he was faltering.

"I like your sister, too."

They grew silent again. Hospital sounds crept up on Tucker. Beeps of monitors. Swishes of machines. The scuffing sound of nurses' rubber-soled shoes. Hushed conversations.

And here he was in a tuxedo.

They stopped at an elevator and Billy pushed the button. The doors opened. As they entered, Billy hit the light for the second floor.

He cleared his throat. "So you're what? Sixteen?"

"Not quite sixteen."

"Do you have plans for college?"

He snorted derisively. "To do what? Move away like Vivi did?" He shook his head. "I know she had her reasons for wanting to leave. But around here, unless you're going to be a teacher, you're better off getting some experience as a construction worker or miner."

"Is that what you want?"

Billy glared at him as if he were crazy. "What I want is to live near my family. No fancy college degree is going to help me do that."

The elevator bell pinged. They headed to the cafeteria in silence. He poured the coffees from tall containers at a drink station and retrieved sufficient sugar and cream for an army as Billy grabbed a soda and two waters. He paid for it with a bank card and they returned to the elevator, where they were silent. With the exception of telling Billy he liked his sister, he seemed to always say the wrong thing.

They finally reached the waiting room. He handed Olivia's parents their coffee. Billy gave him one of the waters. Everyone said thanks and the room grew stone-cold silent again. For an hour.

Thirsty, he'd guzzled his water then wished he hadn't because now he had nothing to do with his hands.

When the doctor finally walked into the room, everybody jumped off their seats.

The doctor held up his hand when everybody but Tucker began to talk at once. "She's fine. Great actually. We had to put a few pins in her leg, and she'll be closely monitored for the next twenty-four hours, but I'm very optimistic. There weren't any internal injuries and her head CT came back normal."

Olivia's mother dissolved into tears. Olivia fell to a chair. Her dad shook hands with the doctor, who left.

After drying her tears, Olivia's mom caught her hand. "You should go home. Change." She laughed a little. Skimming the hem of the poofy skirt of Olivia's dress she said, "This is a pretty little thing."

She smiled across the waiting room at Tucker. "Tucker bought it for me."

Her mother's gaze took a slower, more serious stroll across the room, latching on to his. "Really?"

He'd never realized mothers could be so protective, so suspicious of even simple things, but there was no denying the look on Loraina's face. "Your daughter was responsible for the first showing of a very important new artist in Bordighera, Italy. As an employee of Inferno, she needed to look the part."

"Fancy."

"I wish you could have been there, Mom. It was great. The artist is Antonio Signorelli. His work is fantastic. His dad wanted to foot the bill for a showing so I had to work with him and a woman who owns the gallery and keep Antonio from freaking out." Her eyes grew soft, dreamy. "It was great. The most fun I've ever had."

Her mom clutched her hand. "That does sound great."

She rubbed her fingers along the flounce of her skirt. "Bet I look silly."

"No, you just look like a concerned sister." She glanced at Billy. "But I think Billy should go home. And you, too. And your boss." She said boss in the oddest way, a way that made Tucker feel totally unwelcome. "Get changed. Get some rest. Dad and I will stay. When she wakes up, we'll call you and you can come back to see her."

Rising, Olivia nodded. She hugged her mother and dad, and collected Billy and they headed out of the room.

Tucker caught her hand, if only because he needed to feel her again when she was relieved, happy. "So, all this is good news."

She smiled up at him. "Yes."

Billy made a snorting noise.

Tucker decided to ignore him. He wasn't quite sixteen. His sister had nearly died. His other sister, someone he clearly loved and missed, was home for a few days. He was bound to be a little emotional.

When they arrived at the Prentiss residence, an old two-story house that had a well-kept front yard and blooming flower beds, Tucker brought their suitcases inside. Olivia put on jeans and a T-shirt but Tucker had only dress pants and white shirts. Laughing at him, she drove him to the local discount department store. He didn't wear his tie or jacket but when he walked into the store in black tuxedo trousers and a white silk shirt, he knew he looked silly.

They found jeans and T-shirts and he bought two of each. They checked out and stopped at a fast-food restaurant next door to buy dinner.

She was happy and sweet with her brother as

they ate. But after they returned to her parents' house and he changed into the one of the jeans and T-shirts, right before his eyes, she seemed to wind down.

"You need to go to bed."

She yawned. "I want to stay up so I can go to the hospital when my sister wakes up."

"How about if you sleep and I wake you?"

"How about if we both sleep and put the cell phone on my pillow so we can hear it when she calls?"

She headed toward the stairway which he assumed led to the bedrooms.

Positive he'd heard wrong when she'd said "'we' could hear the alarm," he motioned to the living room. "I guess I'll sleep on the sofa."

She stopped, turned. "I was hoping you'd come upstairs with me."

Everything inside him spiked. Their eyes met. He knew what a huge deal this was for her. A sign of trust. He'd like nothing better than to sleep with her, not for sex but for connection. He didn't want to be separated. He didn't want her to be alone. He didn't want to feel alone, ostracized.

But these profound feelings ignited his desire for her, a desire so intense that he didn't trust himself.

"I can't sleep in your bed."

She took a step toward him. "I promise to be good."

He laughed. "I don't."

She looked up. Time seemed to stop again. "It's okay." She drew in a slow breath. "It's what I want. I need to be close to you."

The words humbled him. He'd never had anybody need him, depend on him for anything other than money or work. Still, he also knew it was wrong. He didn't want to mention the past. He didn't want to bring up the worst time of her life. But he had to get them to slow down again or they'd both regret it.

"If and when we make love, I want it to be slow, special. Not a frenzy of emotion neither one of us can control."

She licked her lips, looked like she would argue, but she finally said, "Okay."

"So I'll sleep on the couch."

"What if we both sleep on the couch?"

Relief sliced through him. He glanced into the living room at the oversize floral sofa. "It's big enough for two people."

"And with Billy roaming around there's no privacy." She walked her hands up his T-shirt. "So you'd have to be on your best behavior."

"I would." As he said the words, he contradicted them by kissing her. The sensations that wove through him awed him. He didn't just like this woman. He'd swear he loved her. Even though he wasn't entirely sure what love was, this new feeling that overwhelmed him couldn't be anything less serious than love.

She slid her hands around his neck, pulling him closer and he deepened the kiss, even as his chest tightened and his breathing grew shallow. A month ago, he'd never thought any further with a woman than lust. Today he wanted everything.

She broke the kiss, took his hand and led him to the sofa. He sat first, reclined and patted the space in front of him. She lay down beside him, spoon fashion.

Wonder trembled through him. He was in love with a woman who was equal parts remarkable and vulnerable. Beautiful and kind. Someone who'd been hurt enough that her mother still behaved like a panther protecting a cub.

And as much as he knew he was in love with her, he also realized he didn't know the first thing about loving her.

CHAPTER FOURTEEN

TUCKER FELL INTO A DEEP sleep. What seemed like only seconds later, the sound of a door closing woke him and he bolted up on the sofa. Rays of the sun poured in through the shear curtains. Olivia's mom stood in the doorway to the living room, her arms crossed on her chest.

"Good morning."

Olivia bounced up in front of him." Good morning, Mom. Sorry." She winced. "This isn't what it looks like."

"Uh-huh."

She said, "Is Cindy awake?" But before her mom could answer she added, "Of course she is or you wouldn't be home. Why didn't you call us?"

"She woke in the middle of the night. The nurses fussed and she couldn't really talk so we decided to let you all get a good night's sleep." Her gaze drifted to Tucker. "She'll be awake again this morning. You can go to the hospital now."

Olivia jumped off the couch. "Let me get a shower and change."

With that she bounded out of the room and Tucker found himself alone with her mom. Seconds noisily ticked off a grandfather clock in the corner. Neither said anything.

Finally, Loraina turned to leave the living room. "I'll make some coffee."

He ran his fingers through his hair. She thought the worst. She had from the moment he'd walked into the hospital waiting room with Olivia. If she were anyone other than Vivi's mom, he wouldn't care. But he did care. He had to care.

He rose and made his way to the kitchen where Loraina stood by a counter preparing coffee.

They were silent for several minutes. When he couldn't take the quiet anymore, he said, "Nothing happened last night."

She didn't even turn from the coffeemaker. "Of course not. I trust my daughter."

He leaned against the counter. "So do I."

She whipped around to face him. "Oh, do you now? You think that means something. That *you* trust her? My daughter's a sweet, precious woman."

"I know how sweet and wonderful she is. In these past few weeks, she's been very good for me."

She sniffed a laugh. "I'm sure she has but are you good for her?"

The kitchen door swung open and Olivia entered. Her hair wet and a big purse over her shoulder. She'd obviously taken the fastest shower in recorded history. "I grabbed a few things that Cindy might want."

"Did you get her iPod?"

"Doesn't she have her phone?"

Her mom shook her head. "It was lost in the accident. I'm going into town this afternoon to get her a replacement with her old number. But if she wakes I think she'd like to at least have her music."

Olivia turned. "I'll get the iPod."

When the door closed behind her, the kitchen became silent again and stayed silent. What could he say to persuade the mother of the woman he had fallen in love with that he was good for her? Should he tell her he'd given her a job? Was helping her start a business? He didn't know much about mothers but he didn't think this one cared about jobs. Especially since the very doubt she was expressing was the same doubt he had himself.

She handed a cup of coffee to him just as Olivia returned to the kitchen.

"Bring that with you," Olivia said, pointing at his coffee. "I want to get going. In fact, I was thinking we should grab breakfast at the hospital and eat in the waiting room."

When they got into the rental car, Olivia took his coffee so he could insert the keys. He wanted the coffee but what he really wanted was a hug and a kiss. He wanted to think she needed them as much as he did. But suddenly everything seemed wrong. Out of place. So he forgot about holding her and the wonderful sensation of having her in his arms, turned the key and got them on the road. Then he took back the coffee.

"A little desperate for caffeine?"

"Actually I'm starving."

"We'll get something as soon as we check on Cindy." She directed him to make two turns that took him to a highway that took them to the hospital.

As he drove, he sipped the coffee which was strong but surprisingly good. When he parked the car, she hopped out. He guzzled the rest of the delicious coffee, left the mug in the car's cup holder and followed her.

The information desk directed them to the ICU where her dad awaited. He hugged Olivia, then smiled at Tucker.

Tucker stepped back, wondering if he'd be smiling after his wife told him he'd slept with his little girl on their sofa.

Though nothing had happened, he knew Vivi's story. Knew that these were the people who'd loved her through the attack that had nearly resulted in a rape. They were protective and to them he was a predator.

"The nurses were taking her vitals, so I came out. You can go in when they give us the all clear."

They sat quietly on plastic seats in a small waiting room. Tucker leaned back, trying not to feel out of place, unwanted. When the nurse came in, Olivia jumped up. "Let's go."

He hesitated. Everything that had happened in the past few days suddenly seemed surreal. Not only did he believe he had fallen in love, but Olivia's family didn't like him. And now he was being invited to the ICU bed of her sister.

At the very worst possible time in their lives, he'd nudged his way into this family without a second thought.

And he hadn't for one minute felt he belonged here.

"Coming?"

He rose from his seat but didn't take the steps to the door. "You go."

Her head tilted. "What?"

"I'm a complete stranger and your sister is very sick. She doesn't want a stranger at her bedside. You go alone." He turned to her father. "Or let your dad go back in."

Her father's eyes lit with agreement, so Tucker sat again. They left the waiting room and he watched the door to the ICU swallow them up.

Then he sat back, closed his eyes.

He didn't belong here.

Vivi stepped inside the small curtained-off area where her sister lay. Her breath stalled when she saw the cuts and bruising and the metal thing around her leg that connected to pulleys and kept it elevated.

"My God, she looks terrible."

"The nurses tell us she's actually doing very well. In a few days her pain killers will be reduced. She'll be awake longer than two minutes and she'll be able to talk to us."

She walked to the bed, slid her hand along the cool sheet. "So this is good?"

Her dad smiled. "Very good. We'll take it one day at a time. You just have to be patient."

"Oh, I'm the most patient in the land."

"Yes, you are." He walked over and surprised her by enveloping her in a hug. "We've always been proud of you."

"Yeah, well, this morning Mom might not agree. She came home and found Tucker and me sleeping on the couch."

Her dad frowned. "I thought he was your boss."

"He's a little more than my boss, Dad."

Her dad's mouth fell. "Oh, Vivi. After everything you've been through, please do not tell me you'd get involved with a guy who would—" he paused, as if trying to figure out what to say and finally settled on "—use you."

Vivi gasped. "He would never use me!"

"Really? Big-city guy like that? A guy with money? A guy accustomed to getting what he wants and then walking away when he grows tired? You're sure he won't use you?"

She groped for something to say, something that would make him see that Tucker wasn't using her, but when she went back over all their time together, she couldn't really think of anything definitive. Everything they did together somehow involved work. Lots of it even involved him getting a shot at Constanzo's company.

She swallowed then shook her head to clear it. So much had happened in the past few days that her thinking was muddled. She knew Tucker. Better than anybody.

"He's a good guy, Dad. And I won't do anything stupid."

"Okay." He laughed nervously and brushed his fingers along the back of his neck. "You I trust. Him not so much. You just keep a good head on your shoulders."

She stayed the fifteen minutes she was allowed then walked out of the ICU with her dad. When they returned to the waiting room, they found Tucker and her mom sitting silently.

Loraina rose. "Your shift is over," she said with a smile before placing a kiss on her dad's cheek.

"Are you sure you want to stay all day?"

"I feel lucky getting days, since you're stuck with nights."

Her dad wrapped his arms around her mom's waist. "I don't mind."

It was the kind of exchange Olivia had seen every day of her life. Simple, normal, day-to-day love. She glanced at Tucker and saw he'd looked away.

The odd feeling tumbled through her again, making her stomach queasy. She'd worried at Antonio's party that they were taking things too fast, worried that he might only want sex from her. In her desperate need for connection the night before, she'd even offered herself to him, but he'd been a gentleman. In the light of day, though, everything looked different. She was working her way into his world. But he seemed nervous in hers—as if he didn't want to be here.

"You go home, too, Vivi."

When Tucker heard those words coming from Loraina, he almost jumped off his chair, eager to leave this quiet, tense place. But he caught himself and rose slowly. Olivia may not want to leave.

"We don't want to go, Mom. We'll keep you company."

She glanced at Tucker. "Are you sure?"

Olivia said, "Yeah. Cindy's doing fine. But we all want to be here for her."

He started to sit again, but Loraina gave him another one of her looks and he stopped himself. They didn't need him. They didn't want him. He was absolutely in the way. And seeing Olivia's life up close and personal, he understood why Loraina had asked him if he was good for her.

He wasn't. Olivia might know just the right words to say to him to make him happy, or comfortable, but he didn't know what to say to her. They'd really only "talked" for two weeks—and that was on the phone. They'd "been in love" one day—a little over twenty-four hours. He needed to give her space and maybe he needed a little more time to think all this through.

"Maybe I should just go."

Olivia's gaze jumped to his. "Go?"

"Yeah. There's really nothing for me to do here. And I probably have eight zillion emails."

"Really? You're leaving for emails?"

He glanced at her mom, then back at her. "You guys need your privacy."

Her eyes dulled. She smiled shakily. "You're fine here with us."

"I'm in the way."

She studied him a few seconds then said, "You know what? Let's take a walk."

He motioned for her to precede him and when they got far enough away from the waiting room she said, "What's really going on?"

"Olivia, your family is in crisis. I have huge, wonderful enormous feelings for you, but I don't belong here."

"Of course, you do!"

"Olivia, take a look at your parents. They don't want me here."

"I'll talk to them."

His heart skipped a beat. "No! My God, their daughter is lying in a hospital bed. If I leave, the extra stress I add will go and you won't have to talk to them."

Even as he said the words, new fear tightened his chest. What if something he said, something he did, put a wedge between her and her family? What if being with him took away the thing she had that he'd always longed for: a family?

"I need you here."

He shook his head. "No, you don't. You need your family. And they need you."

Suddenly they were at the elevator. Considering it a sign, he pressed the button. She walked over to him, placed her hands on his chest in a gesture he was coming to expect from her, something that made him feel he was hers. Special, precious to her. Her parents might not like him but she did. A lot. She might even love him.

But he'd lived through the last twenty-four hours with her. The best he'd done was get her to this hospital. He hadn't known words of consolation. Didn't fit into her family. Hell, the truth of it was, he might not fit into *any* family. And the very worst possibility was that his inability to fit might drive a wedge between her and the family she adored. The family who adored her.

No matter how he analyzed this, he wasn't good for her.

"Of course, I need my family. But I'd also like you to be here."

He clasped her hands and inched them away from his chest. "Don't you see how different we are?"

"Yes. We both saw it from the day we met. That doesn't mean we're wrong for each other."

He drew in a slow breath. Closed his eyes then popped them open again. Though it shredded his very needy heart to say it, he knew it was the right thing to do. "Yes. It does."

Her eyes filled with tears. "No! It doesn't!"

He realized then how much she cared for him. He also knew that with her sister struggling, she wasn't thinking logically. He had to be the strong one. The smart one. The brave one. Because without her, he had nothing. But without him, she still had family. A brother. A sister. A mom. A dad. A brand-new career in a world full of people who would love her. People she'd get along with easily. Not someone she'd have to struggle with the way she always struggled with him.

"I have to go. I'm not letting any grass grow under my feet with Constanzo."

The elevator pinged. The doors opened. She stared at him with a look of complete confusion.

He almost said, "I love you. I honestly believe

you are the first person I've ever loved. And I will miss you so much that I may always feel it."

But, in the end, he knew that it would hurt her or give her false hope about a relationship that was bad for her. So he walked onto the elevator, hit the down button and refused to look at her as the doors closed behind him.

CHAPTER FIFTEEN

VIVI STARED AT the elevator door shell-shocked. He wasn't just leaving. In the space of twenty-four hours of being with her family he'd decided they didn't belong together.

That she wasn't good enough.

She tried to tell herself that was wrong. But as she made her way through the day, keeping up appearances for her family who had enough to worry about, she realized she'd dragged him to a backward small town, made him buy jeans at a discount store and promised him a breakfast he hadn't gotten.

All while her disapproving parents looked on.

What if seeing her roots, where she'd come from, who she really was, had shown him the real her? What if he'd been looking at her through rose-colored glasses, thinking she was something she wasn't...or what if all this time he'd actually been making her into the woman he'd wanted her to be?

Pain gripped her heart, stopped her breathing.

Just as he was revamping Jason Jones, he'd been revamping her, creating his perfect woman. He'd eased her into a whole new career, bought her a dress that turned her into a socialite look-alike. Of course he was changing her into the woman he wanted her to be.

She was such a fool not to see it. He didn't love her. He loved the woman he was turning her into.

Her dad wasn't right, but he wasn't wrong either. Tucker might not be the kind of guy who would use her and then dump her. But he was the kind of guy to take someone with potential and turn them into what he needed.

Now that he'd seen the real her, her real life, her roots, he'd probably realized the changes wouldn't stick. And she knew he wouldn't be coming back.

She'd lost him.

If she'd ever really had him—and she didn't think she had. He loved the woman he'd been making her into. Not her.

Tears filled her eyes and she let them fall. She'd almost made as a big of a mistake with him as she had with Cord.

Tucker flew back to Italy and made arrangements for Constanzo to send a car to his private airstrip for him. Though he couldn't sleep or work on the flight, he refused to think about Olivia. He wouldn't even consider that he had abandoned her because he hadn't. She had loving parents, a little brother who wasn't so little and a sister who would soon be leaning on her. She didn't need him. But even if she had, he would have screwed it up. She needed, *deserved,* someone she could depend on, someone she could trust. He was not that guy.

And her parents had seen that.

He walked down the steps, out of his plane and over to the limo. The driver opened the door and when he slid inside he kicked Constanzo's ankles.

"Constanzo? You didn't have to meet me. I would have been fine traveling to your house alone."

"Why are you here?"

"To negotiate, remember?" He scowled. "Unless you're backing out of our deal."

"I don't back out of deals. But you shouldn't be here. Vivi is in trouble and you are here with me…talking business."

"I don't want any grass to grow under our feet."

"You are deserting her!"

"I'm not!"

He wasn't sure how the shout had escaped but it infuriated him. He was better than this. Smarter than this. He'd fallen in love with a woman who deserved a better partner than he could be. It broke his heart. But he had to move on. He couldn't shout or scream or rail at the unfairness of it. He had to move on.

He drew a long slow breath, reaching for his trademark calm. "I'm sorry."

"I'm not. It's the first real emotion you've ever shown around me." He sniffed a laugh. "Unless one counts the emotion I see on your face when you look at Vivi."

He turned his head, glanced out the window, unable to hold Constanzo's gaze anymore.

"You love her."

"It doesn't matter. I'm not good for her. I don't fit in her family. Worse, her family's in crisis and I froze."

"So?"

"So?" He gaped at Constanzo. "So she needed somebody strong and reliable and I had no clue what to say or do. I'm damaged. You know that. I didn't have a normal family life."

"There is no such thing as a normal family life. And I'm sure no one expected you to be strong or reliable. They just wanted you there."

He snorted. "Trust me. They didn't."

Constanzo drew back. "Are you whining?"

"I'm not whining. I'm facing truth. She has a sweet, wonderful family. I grew up in foster homes with moms who made me pack my own lunch and sometimes cook my own dinner. No one ever talked to me about life. I had to figure out personal hygiene from books. I don't know anything about real bonds. While Olivia's family kisses and hugs and talks, I have no idea how to relate to them."

"Tucker! You spent about ten hours with them! You've only known Olivia six or eight weeks. Getting along with people, even the woman you love takes time. Did you think this would be easy?"

"I—" Falling for Olivia had been easy. Natural. Her parents were a totally different story. "I don't want to be so much at odds with her parents that I put a wedge between her and her family. I don't want her to lose what I never had. That would be the ultimate selfishness."

"You won't take her away. You will learn to get along with them."

"Right."

"When you first met Vivi, you didn't know how to deal with her."

He said nothing. But remembered how awkward she'd made him feel.

"But eventually you figured it out."

"She forced me to figure it out."

"She'll help you fit."

"She shouldn't have to help me fit." Hatred of his start in life rolled through him on a hot ball of anger. All he'd ever wanted was to be normal and he'd figured out how. How to be bold and wise and never let anyone take advantage of him. None of that worked in a family.

"Weren't you helping her fit into your world?"

"Yes. But that's different."

"Why?"

"Because my world isn't something everybody understands. Family life is."

"Oh, Tucker. You are making a huge mistake. Go back. Try. Otherwise, you'll be me in thirty years. Except I don't think you have an illegitimate son to find. Someone to give your life meaning. Do you want to be me? Searching out people like you and Vivi who keep you company only because they sort of have to?"

The picture that came to mind surprised him. It wasn't a vision of himself thirty years from now. It was a vision of himself thirty days from now when he returned to his sterile penthouse. Alone. His cold office. Empty. Without even the chance of seeing Olivia in the halls of Inferno because she would be globe-hopping with Antonio. Or looking for new clients. Or going to galleries, studying the art.

Without him.

And he'd even be paying for it.

"You have a chance for a whole new life. You simply have to face a few weeks of mistakes as you adjust to having a family." He leaned across the seat and squeezed Tucker's hand. "A real family. Your family, if you marry her."

He sniffed a laugh. "She already asked me to marry her once."

Constanzo laughed with delight. "She's a girl who knows what she wants and goes after it.

Maybe you should take a page from her." He patted Tucker's knee. "Get back on the plane. Humble yourself a little bit. The world is at your feet. A real life is at your feet. Not just Olivia's mom and dad and sister and brother...but kids. Your kids. A dark-haired boy. A strawberry blonde little girl."

He swallowed. He could picture it. He could actually see himself at a swing set. Or teaching his kids to swim. Or taking them to the opera and tickling them awake when they fell asleep. He could see Vivi running a household and having a career. He could see himself slowing down. Traveling with her. Sharing her exciting new career.

"Go home, Tucker. We can talk deal anytime. Right now Vivi needs you."

As if the driver had been listening in on their conversation, the limo door opened.

He stared at it, for the first time in his life seeing freedom and happiness only a few steps away.

A few steps and an eight-hour flight.

Followed by a two-hour drive.

And even those could be a waste if Constanzo was wrong and Vivi didn't want him. Didn't trust him to help her through this. Didn't trust him with her heart.

Two days later, Vivi left the hospital with her head down. They'd had a good day. Cindy had laughed—though it had caused her ribs to hurt so they'd upped her pain meds and she'd fallen back into a deep sleep and hadn't again awakened for hours.

Which had been very bad for Vivi. Because when the room was quiet, she had plenty of time to think about Tucker.

She couldn't believe she'd been so foolish as to fall for him, to believe he was different, that he'd love her in spite of her flaws, her wounds. But the ache in her very soul was proof that she had been. She'd fallen in love with a man who didn't love. He changed people. Molded them to be what he wanted so he didn't have to change.

Oh, she understood why. His upbringing had made him cautious and aware that people could hurt him. So he played it safe all the time.

But hadn't she proven she'd never hurt him?

Even if she had, he hadn't paid attention. He'd still tried to change her. Tried to make her into his perfect woman. He didn't want her. He wanted someone he thought was perfect.

She reached the curb, lifted her head to look both ways before crossing the parking lot and stopped dead in her tracks. A few feet in front of her, leaning against a beat-up rental car, wearing the discount department-store jeans, was Tucker. He had his arms crossed on his chest, his butt on the car's hood and his legs extended as if he'd been waiting a long time.

She started walking again, heading for her own car, determined to ignore him, but—

Well, there wasn't any reason for him to accidentally be in Kentucky. He'd come to see her. And, damn it, if the flutter of her heart was anything to go by, she desperately wanted him to have come back to her. The real her. Not his perfect woman, but the woman with a sister in the hospital, parents who were worried and a sarcastic little brother.

She changed directions and walked toward him. He lifted himself from the hood.

"I'm sorry."

She smiled slightly, not sure how to take that. Was he sorry he'd left? Sorry he'd tried to change her? Or did he feel what she'd felt? That walking away had torn out his soul.

She'd spent every minute of their time together giving him the benefit of the doubt, believing the best about him, only to be hurt. She couldn't believe the best this time, couldn't make excuses for him. He had to speak. And he had to say the right things.

She looked across the parking lot, at the green, tree-covered mountains behind him. "I think you're going to have to do better than that."

"Sorry's not good enough?"

"Nope."

"Not even from someone who loves you?"

Though her heart raced and her arms longed to swing around him and hold him close so he could never get away, she said, "You don't love me. Otherwise, you wouldn't have gone."

"I left because I love you so much I think you deserve better."

She sniffed a laugh. "Right. That's why you tried to change me."

"Change you?"

"You elevated me from meager accountant to manager, someone who can be seen in public with you. Especially in a five-thousand-dollar designer dress. Something I couldn't have afforded for myself but something appropriate for me to be seen in with you. Almost as if I wasn't good enough the way I was."

"Oh, Olivia. Oh, God. Is that how you saw that?"

Her lips trembled but she continued to gaze off into the distance. He put his fingers on her chin, forcing her to look at him, reminding her of the first time he'd touched her and how she'd known, in that very second, that there was something different about him...about them.

"I wasn't trying to change you. Just help you. I would put the world at your feet if I thought you wanted it." He sucked in a breath. "You're perfect, wonderful. Just the way you are. I'm the problem here."

"You?"

"Your family loves you. Stands by you. Acts a bit like a bunch of barracudas assigned to protect you. And I'm…broken, Olivia. I'm the one who might not be good enough for you."

"But you love me?"

"Yes. Scarily. I want you—want a relationship with you—so badly that it terrifies me."

Her lips quirked. "I think if you do it right, love's supposed to be scary."

He barked a laugh. "What?"

"Well, people in love share secrets, form bonds, sacrifice." She smiled. "You've been spoiled a long time."

His hands slid to her waist. "Spoiled?"

She stepped closer. "Buying yourself everything you wanted."

He laughed, nestled her against him. "I have."

"But you couldn't buy me."

He grew serious. "I know."

"Yet you still won me."

He caught her gaze. "Have I?"

"Oh, come on. Where's the great Tucker Engle, guy who sees all, knows all?"

He smiled. "You love me."

"So you'll win over my parents. You'll make mistakes. Occasionally, you'll say you're sorry."

He winced.

She playfully slapped his arm. "Saying you're sorry isn't that hard."

"I don't know. Your mother's a tough cookie."

She laughed. "Kiss me, you idiot. We're going to make this work."

He kissed her then and she melted against him. Because they were going to make this work. Not just because she loved him but because they were good together, honest, in the way people who'd had softer, easier lives couldn't be. They'd appreciate every minute of every day together, have kids, build a family.

And he'd never be alone again.

EPILOGUE

WHEN THE LIMO pulled up to Constanzo's home, Olivia raced to meet it. She didn't wait for the driver to come around to open the door, she opened it herself.

"Welcome to Italy, Mom and Dad!"

Her dad slid out of the limo first then reached in to help her mom out. "Beautiful place. The trees remind me of home."

She hugged him, then her mom. "I thought the same thing."

Her mom glanced around. "I can see why you'd want to get married here."

Cindy ran out the front door with a squeal. As maid of honor and groomsman, she and Billy had arrived a week early to help with preparations. "I'm so glad you're here."

Her mom caught her in a hug. "Have you been making Billy mind?"

Cindy pulled away with a laugh, her short curly blond hair bouncing in the breeze.

Olivia said, "He's eighteen, Mom. Cut the apron

strings. This fall, he'll be attending college in New York, living in his own apartment."

"Only a few floors down from us," Tucker said, coming out to greet her parents. He hugged her mom, shook hands with her dad. "We won't let things get out of hand."

Behind the scenes the driver unloaded their bags. Tucker directed them into the house. Constanzo stood in the foyer, waiting for them.

"Loraina! Jim! I finally get you to my home."

Jim shook his hand. "Hey, you've never come to Kentucky. I still owe you for beating me at pool at Tucker's."

"I happen to have a pool table in the den."

Olivia sighed. "We're here for a wedding. Not a pool tournament. Tucker, tell them no tournaments."

He said, "No tournaments," but he laughed.

Olivia took her mom's arm. "What do you want to see first? The pool? Your room? Antonio's studio?"

"Oh, I don't want to disturb Antonio."

Antonio walked up the hall, drying his hands on a cloth. "You won't disturb me." He walked over and kissed Loraina. "You're my biggest fan. You never disturb me."

"Then give me ten minutes to get out of my traveling clothes and we'll go to your studio."

Cindy said, "I think I'm going to help the cook with lunch."

Jim sidled up to Constanzo. "Once I change I'll meet you at that pool table."

"I will be there."

In seconds, everybody had scattered, leaving Tucker and Olivia alone in the foyer.

"If you want, I can scold them about playing pool."

She smiled. "No. Let them." She glanced off in the direction Constanzo had hustled. "It's nice to see them getting along."

"It's nice to see us all get along."

She slid her arms around his waist. "People are people. Give us enough time and we can all find common ground."

"Speaking of common ground." He placed his hand on her tummy. "Have you told your parents yet about the ultimate common ground?"

She laughed. "No. I thought we'd get through the wedding first then tell them they're going to be grandparents. One exciting step at a time."

He kissed her. "One happy step at a time."

"Yeah. One happy step at a time."

* * * * *

COMING NEXT MONTH FROM

 HARLEQUIN®

Romance

Available March 4, 2014

#4415 THE RETURNING HERO
by Soraya Lane
When soldier Brett Palmer, Jamie's late husband's best friend, turns up on her doorstep, she *knows* it's fate. Could this be the second chance they've both been looking for?

#4416 ROAD TRIP WITH THE ELIGIBLE BACHELOR
by Michelle Douglas
When an airline strike interferes with their plans, Quinn Laverty reluctantly embarks on a road trip with (gorgeous!) politician Aidan. But will this be the most unexpected and life-changing journey of their lives?

#4417 SAFE IN THE TYCOON'S ARMS
by Jennifer Faye
Kate Whitley has asked for billionaire Lucas's help, and he can't refuse this beautiful stranger. Will this be the woman to see behind the headlines...and into his heart?

#4418 AWAKENED BY HIS TOUCH
by Nikki Logan
Corporate realizer Elliot may be on Laney's doorstep strictly for business, but as he begins to see life through her eyes, the chemistry between them becomes impossible to ignore....

YOU CAN FIND MORE INFORMATION ON UPCOMING HARLEQUIN® TITLES, FREE EXCERPTS AND MORE AT WWW.HARLEQUIN.COM.

HRLPCNM0214

"LET ME STAY for a few days, let you catch up on some sleep while I'm here."

His voice was lower than usual, an octave deeper. She shook her head. "You don't have to do that. I'll be fine."

She might have been telling him no, but inside she was screaming out for him to stay. Having Brett here would make her feel safe, let her relax and just sleep solidly for a few nights at least, but she didn't expect him to do that.

And her intentions weren't pure, either. Because ever since she'd starting thinking about Brett in a certain way last night, remembering how soft his lips had been, how sensual it had been pressed against his body, she'd thought of nothing other than having him here. Keeping him close. Wondering if something could happen between them, and whether he wanted it as much as she did, even if she did know it was wrong.

"If I'm honest, Brett, having you here for a few days sounds idyllic." She wanted to stay strong, but she also wanted a man in her house again. Wanted the company of someone she could actually talk to, who wasn't afraid of the truth. Of what had happened to her husband. Because she had no one else to talk to, and no one else to turn to. She'd lost her dad and then her husband to war, and she was tired of being alone. "But only if you're sure."

She listened to Brett's big intake of breath, watched the way his body stiffened, then softened back to normal again.

"Then I'll stay. As long as you need me here, I'll stay."

She dropped her head to his shoulder. "He would have liked you being here. You know that, right?"

Brett shrugged, but she could tell he was finding this as awkward as she was. "You know, he made me promise to look out for you if anything ever happened to him. I just never figured that we'd actually be in that position."

Jamie smiled. "I'll never forget what you've done for me, Brett."

Brett was her friend. Nothing more. She just had to keep reminding herself of that, because falling in love with her husband's best buddy? Not something that could happen. Not now, not ever.

Brett could have been the man of her dreams—*once*. But now wasn't the time to look back. Now was about the future. The one she had to build without her husband by her side. No matter how much she was thinking about *that* kiss.

Don't miss THE RETURNING HERO by Soraya Lane, available March 2014. And look out for the second in this heartwarming duet, HER SOLDIER PROTECTOR, available April 2014.